Irish Chain

Barbara Haworth-Attard

IRISH CHAIN

HarperTrophyCanada™
An imprint of HarperCollinsPublishersLtd

Irish Chain
© 2002 by Barbara Haworth-Attard. All rights reserved.

Published by Harper*Trophy*Canada™,
an imprint of HarperCollins Publishers Ltd

Harper*Trophy*Canada™ is a trademark of HarperCollins Publishers.

First published in trade paperback by Harper*Trophy*Canada™,
an imprint of HarperCollins Publishers Ltd, 2002.
This mass market paperback edition 2004.

HarperCollins books may be purchased for educational, business,
or sales promotional use through our Special Markets Department.

HarperCollins Publishers Ltd
2 Bloor Street East, 20th Floor
Toronto, Ontario, Canada
M4W 1A8

www.harpercanada.com

National Library of Canada Cataloguing in Publication

Haworth-Attard, Barbara, 1953–
Irish chain / Barbara Haworth-Attard. – Mass market pbk. ed.

ISBN 0-00-639216-4

I. Title.

PS8565.A865I75 2004   jC813'.54   C2003-905648-1

OPM 9 8 7 6 5 4 3 2 1

Printed and bound in the United States
Set in Monotype Plantin Light

In memory of my Irish grandmother,
Rose (Neeson) Haworth
and my Scottish grandmother,
Edna (Conwath) Turner.

And some there be, which have no memorial; who
   perished, as though they had never been . . .
But these were merciful men, whose righteousness
   hath not been forgotten . . .
Their bodies are buried in peace; but their name
   liveth for everymore.

Ecclesiasticus, Chapter 44

Contents

Chapter 1

"Rose! Get stirring yourself, girl." Mam's voice floated up the stairs from the kitchen to the bedroom, where I stood in front of the small mirror over the dresser.

"She dawdles something awful, Mam." I heard my sister Winnifred's voice. "Can't I go on ahead without her? The Sisters don't like us being late."

"No. You wait for Rose. You're too young to be travelling the streets on your own. There are too many strangers around. Halifax has become far too big for itself, what with half the country flocking here for war jobs," Mam told her.

I stirred myself by spitting on my finger, then smoothing an eyebrow. Mam wouldn't approve of a girl spitting, even on her own finger, but Winnie had used all the water in the china jug and I didn't want to go downstairs to refill it. I patted the blue bow in my hair, pleased with myself. I looked half presentable today. Mary had tied my hair up in rags last night and, for a wonder, the curls were staying put. Every one of us had Da's red hair, from Winnie's ginger to Mary's auburn, but mine had to be the brightest. Add to that the raspberry freckles splashed across my nose and . . . well, when God handed out beauty, I must have been at the end of the line—the brains' line too. I have asked Him why that was on a number of occasions, but He's not answered yet.

"Rose!"

Mam was getting annoyed now, but I couldn't seem to move any faster. Winnie was right. I did dawdle, but it was hard to hurry for something you absolutely hated, and I absolutely hated school.

I clattered down the stairs and burst into the kitchen. Mam's face was a picture of vexation.

"Mary curled my hair last night and I had trouble taking the rags out," I explained hurriedly. "But look . . ." I shook my head from side to side. "They're staying in. She set them with sugar water."

Mam raised her eyebrows at that, but thankfully didn't pursue it. "Gather your books up, then, and off you go."

Ernest came up from the basement with a scuttle of coal that he set beside the stove. "Is that enough, Mam?" Without waiting for an answer, he grabbed a cap and rammed it sideways on his head.

"Now, where are you off to in such a hurry?" Mam asked. "It certainly isn't school that has your feet moving so fast."

Since the boys' school burned down, Ernest had attended the girls' school, St. Joseph's. We had classes in the morning, the boys in the afternoon.

"Patrick and me, we're going to the barracks to watch the cadets parade," Ernest said.

Patrick was our cousin from around the corner. What Ernest saw in him, I'll never know. Soft and pudgy, he was a lump of a boy whose main purpose in life seemed to be to hurt anything that got in his way—animal or person. I knew. I had been on the receiving end of his jibes many times. I tried telling myself that was just Patrick, but it still rankled.

"Put that hat on properly. You look like a ruffian," Mam scolded.

Grinning broadly, Ernest yanked open the door and headed out at a run, hat still askew. I grimaced at his departing back. Ernest could get away with almost anything. All he had to do was give his cheeky smile and people forgot his misdeeds. Or maybe it was because he was a boy. It seemed to me boys went through life easy. For some reason God had seen fit to make me a girl. I've asked Him about that, too, but He's not answered yet.

Mam caught my down-turned lips. "You keep that sour look on your face, missy, it might stay that way forever," she warned me.

I hastily straightened my mouth. Red hair, freckles *and* a sour face. I'd be an old maid for sure.

Mam turned to the table. "Oh! Would you just look? Frederick's gone off to work and left his lunch—again. He'd forget his head if the good Lord hadn't attached it to his neck." She pursed her lips. "Well, he can't spend a day on the docks working without a lunch in him. And you know your father—he'd bluster about a bit, then share his own. Then they'd both be hungry. You'll have to take Frederick's lunch to him, Rose."

My stomach tightened.

"Winnie, you will have to walk to school by yourself. Don't talk to anyone," Mam cautioned.

"Not even the other girls?" Winnie asked.

"Of course, you can talk to the other girls. I meant any strangers—grown-up strangers."

Winnie took everything a person said exactly the way they said it. It could be quite bothersome at times.

"If I take Fred's lunch to him, I'll be dreadfully late," I ventured. I didn't like going to the docks. They were noisy and confusing and full of men. "The Sisters will be mad," I added. Not that it mattered. They were always mad with me, anyway. Still, when Sister Frances's ruler came down across a person's knuckles, it hurt for the entire day.

"I'll go, Mam," Winnie offered.

And she would, too. Nothing scared Winnie. She raced around every corner anxious to see what waited for her there.

"The Sisters don't get as mad at me. Just at Rose because she does poorly in school."

Shame washed over me. Winnie was three years younger, yet she was smarter.

"No, Rose will go," Mam said. She handed me

Frederick's lunch. "Tell the Sisters I kept you back for an errand. Now step along smartly. Da said they'd be working at the rail yard. And don't dally down there. So many rough men around these days: sailors and soldiers and the like. But I guess I shouldn't complain. It's the extra work and the extra pay the war's brought that's let us buy our own home." She glanced around the kitchen with satisfaction. "Oh, and Rose, if you see Duncan doing his rounds, would you tell him to stop by? He forgot the cream last delivery. Now, you heard me?"

"Yes, Mam," I replied, swallowing a small lump of hurt. True, I occasionally did forget to do the things Mam asked me. Well, more than occasionally. I'm fine with a single errand, but more than one and I can't seem to keep them straight in my mind. But I'd been trying harder lately, though no one seemed to notice. No one saw the things I did right, just the ones I did wrong.

"Albert!" Mam suddenly exclaimed. "You naughty boy. Get out of my bread dough. I'll give you such a hiding . . ."

I smiled as I thrust my arms into my coat. Mam threatened someone with a good hiding nearly every day, but she'd never touched any of us. Mam loved us all, right from seventeen-year-old Mary down to four-year-old Bertie.

Mary worked as a secretary on a typewriter for a bank in the heart of Halifax. Da was so proud of her, he was fit to burst at times. But then, Mary was a bit of a wonder in our neighbourhood, where most of the girls worked in factories. She left each morning to catch the tram long before Winnie and I kicked the bedcovers off ourselves. Frederick, at sixteen, had been working on the docks with Da these past few months, loading ships with supplies for the war in Europe. He proudly brought home a man's pay at week's end. Ernest was twelve, exactly one year and a day younger than me. People often took us for twins when we were smaller. Winnie, ten, came next. Then there was the baby of the family, Bertie. As I let myself out the door, I heard him squeal happily. Mam hadn't given him a hiding, but a big hug.

I carefully shut the gate and stood looking at our house. Two-storied and wood-framed, it was identical to the others on Albert Street, but, to my eyes, was tidier than the rest. When you had a landlord, you didn't bother to pull weeds from the front garden. Because we owned our house, Da insisted Ernest keep the yard neat and the fence whitewashed. That fence was Da's pride and joy, put up right after he made the first payment on the house. In summer, Mam grew fresh lettuce, peas and beans in the kitchen garden out back.

Downstairs was the parlour, the kitchen, an enclosed back porch, and Mam and Da's bedroom. Upstairs were two bedrooms, one for the girls and one for the boys. All were spotless as Mam was quite house-proud.

The kitchen, warmed by the black coal stove, always smelled of fresh-baked bread. When just Mam, Bertie and I were there, the room seemed huge, but when the entire family sat around the table for supper, it shrunk. Strangely, we could still squeeze in Granny and Grandpa Dunlea, Da's sister Aunt Helen, Uncle Lyle and Patrick, Da's younger brother Uncle James, his new bride Aunt Ida, and there was still room for a neighbour or two to bring their fiddle or pipes for an evening of music. There is a story in the Bible that Father McManus read our class one day, of Jesus feeding a multitude of people with just a few fish and a loaf of bread that kept on multiplying so no one went hungry. I think the walls of our kitchen were the same. They kept growing to let everyone in.

God sure knew how to tell some good stories, and I loved every one I heard. Which was a puzzling thing, because stories are made up of words and, for the most part, I hate words. The Germans might be our enemies in the war, but my own personal enemies were words and letters. I fought them every day at school.

I turned onto Hanover Street and headed downhill toward the rail yard. A heavy rain the night before had left silver puddles on the road. Water dripped from tree branches, lampposts, and telephone and electric wires. A November fog crept up from the harbour to shroud the houses in mist. I shivered as its cold fingers slipped inside my coat. Despite the discomfort, I was enjoying my walk. It was the quiet time of morning when the women cleared the breakfast from tables and tidied beds before they set out for the shops. The dock and factory workers had been a good two hours at their jobs, and the office workers were even now riding trams downtown.

I came to Granny and Grandpa Dunlea's house. Grandpa paced back and forth in front, sucking on his pipe. Granny didn't let him smoke inside.

"Raw today, Rose," he said when he saw me. He hadn't bothered with his false teeth so early in the morning and his mouth caved inward. "Kind of cold that gets into your bones and leaves them aching. I wouldn't be out here, but your granny hates the smell." He waved his pipe in front of me. "Where are you off to?"

I stopped, surprised at the unusual flow of words from Grandpa. He wasn't much of a talker. "I'm taking Fred's lunch to him. He forgot it—again."

One of Granny's hens came from back of the house and strutted between my legs. I picked it up and handed it to Grandpa.

"Thanks, Rose. Blasted things. Always getting out," Grandpa said. He glanced at the house. "Better get moving before your granny sees you."

We exchanged a grin. I knew exactly what he meant. Granny could talk the hind leg off a mule, Mam said, and once Granny got talking, well, Frederick would never get his lunch nor would I get to school. I'd asked

Mam once why Grandpa didn't say much of anything, and she'd laughed. Granny talked so much, she told me, he couldn't fit a word in edgewise. A curtain twitched at an upstairs window in Granny and Grandpa's house, where Aunt Helen, Uncle Lyle and Patrick lived. I broke into a trot and waved goodbye to Grandpa. If there was one person in the world who could talk more than Granny, it was Aunt Helen. Mam often wondered how the two of them sharing the same roof ever got their housework done.

I continued quickly to Veith Street, where I judged it safe to slow and catch my breath. I was far enough away that I could pretend to be out of earshot if Aunt Helen called after me. A steady *clop-clop* and *squeak* of wheels came to me first, then a horse and wagon materialized out of the fog and pulled up beside me.

"Hello, Rose. And top o' the mornin' to ye, as they'd say in old Ireland," a voice called.

"H-hello, Duncan," I said shyly. I could never seem to speak properly when he was around.

Despite being a year older, Duncan MacDonald was Frederick's best friend. He drove the milk delivery wagon for his father's dairy. I wished desperately that something clever to say would come to me, but my mind just didn't work that fast. Now Mary . . . she would have tossed her auburn hair and smiled saucily and asked Duncan what, if anything, a Scots boy would know about Ireland.

"And how are all the Dunleas this fine day?" he asked.

"We're well," I replied, though I knew what Duncan really meant was, *How is Mary?* Everyone knew he'd been sweet on my sister for years, but Mary was keeping company with a clerk from her bank. Horace was his name and his father was the bank manager. Our family had only met Horace the once when he'd come to pick up Mary. He'd driven an automobile that had brought out the entire neighbourhood for a look. But for the life of me, I couldn't see why she preferred that skinny, fussy milksop to Duncan. Duncan, with his black hair and startling blue eyes, could stop any girl's heart. And he was always cheerful, white teeth flashing in a generous smile. But Mary . . . she just muttered something about delivery boys and went out with Horace. I stopped thinking of Mary for a moment as something nagged at the back of my brain.

"Oh!" The word burst out of me as I remembered. I blushed and lowered my voice. "Duncan, be sure you stop at the house. My mother wants to talk to you."

"Uh-oh. That doesn't sound good. I better not keep her waiting, then." He waved, and clucked to the horse. "Get going, you old nag. And, Rose . . ."

I turned back.

"It's been a while since I went, but I think school's the other direction." Duncan grinned widely.

"Fred forgot his lunch," I yelled after him, then

quickly looked around to see if anyone was about. Mam didn't think it proper for girls to shout on the streets.

Duncan raised a hand in farewell, and I continued downhill. A light breeze stirred the hair about my face, carrying the tang of salt water and fish and coal fumes. It also brought a dampness that I knew would flatten my curls. My heart flattened right along with them. Now I'd arrive late at school looking bedraggled with stringy hair and a nose bright red from the cold.

Men's shouts, and the high, frightened cry of a horse floated toward me on the fog. My feet stumbled a bit as I hurried down Barrington Street and past the telegraph office toward the Canadian Government Railroad freight yard. Here the breeze picked up and pulled apart the mist to reveal the chaos of the rail yard and docks.

Men milled about, shirtsleeves rolled to their elbows, caps perched on their heads. Voices shouted and a burst of laughter sailed high over the noise. Boxcars shunted with a teeth-grinding bang, metal scraping over metal. Cigarette smoke tingled my nose. It could be dangerous work at the rail yard. Men had been crushed by falling crates or shifting trains. We children were to take care there. Da cautioned us many times. I looked around wildly. How on earth would I find Da and Fred in this crowd of workers?

"Out of the way," a man growled. I jumped back as he peered at me from behind a wheeled trolley piled high with wooden boxes. "You shouldn't be down here, little girl. You'll get hurt."

"I'm looking for my brother or father," I hurriedly explained.

The man stopped and pulled out a cigarette, scraped a match across a thorny palm and lit the cigarette, all the while studying me. "You must be one of that carrot-topped bunch from Albert Street. Michael Dunlea's pack o' brats."

I nodded, though I didn't much like his description of us. Mam wouldn't, either.

"Your father's unloading a rail car." The man pointed behind us to a line of boxcars.

"Thank you," I said politely. I quickly jumped over a grid of iron train tracks.

"Da," I called.

He wrestled a box out of a railway car onto a wagon, then turned to me. "Rose. What are you doing here? Shouldn't you be in school?" He pulled off his gloves, wiped his forehead with the back of a grimy hand and frowned at me. Da wouldn't hear of any of us playing hooky. He believed in an education for girls right along with the boys.

"Mam sent me with Fred's lunch. He forgot it."

Da shook his head impatiently. "Your brother's far-ther down, trying to get horses out of the train and onto a ship."

I stepped back and looked along the line of boxcars to see Fred struggling to hold a nervous horse in check. "He's having a hard time of it," I said. "I guess they don't want to go to war."

"No more so than the men, but they have to go anyway."

"Da, will Fred ever have to go?"

"Hopefully not. He's needed here on the docks. This is vital war work, too. Not to say he'll never go, but he's two years away from eighteen and there's no sense borrowing trouble."

Maybe I shouldn't borrow trouble, as Da said, but the war had been going on for over three years now. The year 1917 was drawing to a close and no end to the war was in sight.

"Mam says we should pray it is over soon," I said.

"Yes. Well, if your Mam says so, you better do it."

Da didn't like the religion as much as Mam did. He didn't have much use for priests and confession and penance, happy to leave the saving of our souls up to our mother. But if Mam said we were to go to Mass or confession, he'd make us do it. Da turned and picked up another crate. I watched his arm muscles strain as he hoisted it on top of the other box. Da wasn't the tallest man around, but his shoulders were broad and his hands splayed wide could encircle Mam's waist. Mam said our Da was the most handsome man in Halifax, or would be, but for the thinning ginger hair on top of his head. She always added that bit with a laugh and a gentle pat on his bald spot.

The fog vanished as quickly as it had come. A watery sun struggled weakly through high cloud, but held little warmth. I shielded my eyes and looked out over the harbour to where the Dartmouth Ferry was crossing. "There are a lot of ships in today," I said.

Small vessels expertly wove their way between schooners, transports, freighters and merchant ships. The bright red cross painted on the side of a hospital ship reflected vividly against the steel-grey waters. Those ships arrived with grim regularity. I hated to think of all the young men who returned to Canada hurt, or worse, didn't return at all. A blast of a ship's horn made me wince.

"A convoy's getting organized to go overseas," Da said. He pulled out his tobacco pouch and rolled himself a cigarette. "That's where the horses and these supplies are going. It'll be a large one this time. We're losing so many ships to German submarines, they thought they'd send a huge convoy protected by warships. Safety in numbers. But then, I guess I shouldn't be discussing this with you. I don't know if you're really a German spy pretending to be my daughter."

"Da!"

He laughed. "Give me Fred's lunch. I'll hold it back a bit before letting him have it. Make him think he'll have to work all afternoon on an empty stomach." His hazel eyes shone with mischief. "Think he'll learn a lesson, then, Rose?"

I took one last look down the train to my brother. Fred had always been absent-minded. "I don't think I'd count on it, Da."

I continued looking out over the harbour, reluctant to leave for school. I wouldn't want to be going to war, but I couldn't help but wonder about those countries on the other side of the ocean. Did they have trees? Did the air smell different? The globe on Sister Frances's desk had coloured lands broken by blue painted water. Ireland was pink, meaning it was a British possession, as was Canada.

Ireland was where Mam and Da's family originally came from. My Mam's grandmother Rose made the journey to Canada with her children, one of them Mam's mother, in hopes of a better life. I watched a milk-white gull wheel in lazy circles overhead and wondered if it had ever flown to Ireland. Had it looked down on the green fields and hedges I'd heard about so many times in my grandma's stories? Trouble was, I found it hard to believe Ireland was there on the other side of that vast expanse of heaving water. I was, I had long ago decided, one of those people who need to see things for themselves to believe. Still, I mused, I wouldn't half mind being that gull high above the docks.

Da flicked his cigarette end away. "Off to school with you now, my Wild Irish Rose."

I smiled slightly at my father's nickname for me. Why he'd settled on that one I never understood. Ernest, Winnie or Mary—they could be wild, but me? Then again, there probably wasn't a song about a Wild Irish Mary or Ernest or Winnie.

"And Rose . . ." Da's voice stopped me. "I know you find the studying hard, but keep at it. You can do anything you want with a good education. Look at Mary. I always regretted that I left school early, but your grandpa being laid up with no money coming in meant I had to go to work to support the family. I don't blame him, mind you. A body does what a body has to do. But I want you children to have the opportunities I didn't."

I nodded. I'd heard all this from Da before.

"You're a smart girl. You remember that and work hard."

My feet dragged as I left the rail yard and headed up the steep hill toward St. Joseph's School. Da might think I was smart, but I knew better. I was slow—leastways, that's what the Sisters called me. Patrick—he had other, more hurtful names for me.

I knew my ABC's, but couldn't get them to form proper words. I'd stare at them until my eyes watered, willing them to shape themselves into something sensible for me to read, but they never did. It was the same with numbers. I could recite the times tables flawlessly, add and subtract in my head, but when it came time to write them down, I'd mix them all up. I swear that the numbers and letters moved around right in front of my eyes, taunting me.

Sister Frances thought me lazy and inattentive, a daydreamer, she said. I had to admit that sometimes it was easier to gaze out the classroom window than wrestle with my letters. She often made me stay in at the mid-morning break to finish my work. It was embarrassing to be kept in, but worse was the fact that I was the oldest in my class, having been held back twice already. Thank goodness, I'd not grown much yet so I didn't look too much bigger than my classmates, but if I got held back one more year it meant I'd be in Winnie's class. I vow I would quit school before I'd go into Winnie's class.

Breathless from the long climb, I stood and looked up at the two-storey school. I caught my reflection in the glass pane of the door. Sure enough, the wind and damp had flattened my curls and the cold had made my freckles stand out like a measles rash. Unable to put it off any longer, I pulled open the heavy door, walked past the marble statue of the Virgin Mary and climbed the stairs to my classroom.

Chapter 2

A soft murmur filled the school's hallways. Morning prayers were in progress. I stole a look in my classroom door to catch Sister Frances frowning back at me. I shrugged off my coat and hung it in the cloakroom. Head bowed, I slipped into my seat. Already my knuckles stung from the anticipated punishment of her ruler. I clamped my hands together tightly, feeling them sticky with sweat, and mouthed words of devotions repeated so often they came to me without thought.

Immediately after prayers were completed, Sister Frances stomped up and down the row of desks, black habit swirling about her stout legs. "Feet on the floor. Hands palm down on the desk," she ordered.

There was an anxious silence as she checked everyone's fingernails for dirt. Didn't nuns occasionally want to wear something other than the black? I wondered wildly, as Sister neared my desk.

She stopped in front of me. A ruler swung between her thumb and forefinger. My eyes followed its motion.

"You're late," she stated flatly.

I dragged my gaze from the ruler to her ruddy, broad face with its crooked nose and narrow lips. She looked,

I decided, like a man from the docks dressed in nun's clothes. I swallowed that thought with a nervous giggle. "I'm sorry, Sister. My—"

"Stand when you are speaking to me."

I scrambled to my feet. "Sorry, Sister," I apologized a second time. "My mother sent me on an errand. She said you may speak with her about it if you wish," I added. Mam had said no such a thing, so I crossed my fingers behind my back to cancel out the lie. Fibbing is bad at any time, but with a nun standing in front of you, it was probably a terrible sin. I had trouble at times sorting out my sins as to which ones were worse than others. Nervousness prompted my tongue to wag. "My brother, Frederick, he forgot—"

"Never mind. Sit down," Sister Frances ordered. "I would think your parents would have you attend early rather than late, a backward student such as yourself."

My face flooded with colour as a few stifled snickers reached me from the back of the room. I stared down at the scarred desktop. They'd become worse since the boys used our school in the afternoon. The nuns checked the desks each morning before classes for naughty words carved in the wood, and gouged them out. A sort of contest, with the desks as losers.

"Let's see if you've done your homework, class. Get out your readers."

I hastily pulled a book from my bag and opened it to the correct page.

"As you came in late, you may read first, Rose. Stop at the end of the third paragraph."

I stood, took a deep breath and willed my knees to stop knocking. I held the book carefully in front of me and read the page without a single error.

"Stop," Sister Frances ordered. "I said to the end of the third paragraph, but you went on to the fourth. You never listen. That was very good," she added grudgingly. "Now, tell me why you can read well this time, yet yesterday you stumbled all over the words?"

The small relief I'd felt at having done my reading successfully faded rapidly under Sister's questioning stare. I stood dumb, horrified. Truth was, I hadn't read the page at all. Merely recited it. Mary had read it to me the night before, after many pleas on my part, never guessing I was committing it to memory. It was something I had stumbled on about a year ago—this ability to memorize easily. But only one thing at a time. Add more, and confusion set in again.

Suddenly, I realized that this was one of those questions adults don't expect to be answered, and sat down. I hunched my shoulders protectively about my ears and stuck my face inside the book. I pulled my head out once and glanced at the wooden cross hanging on the wall near the picture of the King and Queen. *Please, God, don't let Sister ask me to read again.* Except—was I praying for help with a lie? If so, that would definitely be a sin. Sister said every sin left a black mark on your heart. In that case, I had the blackest heart of any girl in this room.

Somehow, I got through the morning without being called on again. I wasn't sure if that was God's work or not, but I liked to think it was. I was allowed out for mid-morning break, and pulled my coat over my pinafore and went into the yard.

A group of girls from my supposed-to-be-in class stood by the only tree left in the yard. One glanced over at me, caught me staring back and looked immediately away. Martha Schultz. She was my best friend. Or she had been. I wasn't sure what she was these days. Neither she nor I had ever been very popular, but at least last year the other girls would let us stand on the fringes of the group. This year, no one let me stand near or talked to me, not even Martha. I wasn't even popular with the most unpopular girl at school. I've asked God why that was, but He hasn't answered yet. Mam tried to explain one day when I was feeling low. She said Martha was kindly, but had no gumption. Martha couldn't stand up to anyone. I think it was all Catherine's doing. Catherine with her war hero father, her beautiful dresses and glossy chestnut hair that never hung limp.

Mam said God gave every person a burden to carry, and I truly believe Catherine was mine. She had come to our school this past September. She lived with her grandmother and a live-in maid in a large house near

St. Joseph's. She wasn't Catholic, but her grandmother placed her in our school as it was only a few blocks away from their house. Within a couple of days, Catherine had become queen of the playground. She told the girls who they could be friendly with and who not. Suddenly, I found myself a *who not*.

I pushed my back against the school wall and stared over the north end of Halifax, pretending I didn't care that I was alone. Yet I did. So much so that my throat felt tight and sore. My legs shook, too, but I put that down to having read in front of the class.

The sky had cleared now, the last traces of mist and cloud burnt away by a sun so bright it made my head ache and my eyes water. I gazed at the houses and stores tossed together willy-nilly down the hill toward the harbour. Black smoke belched from the chimney of the sugar refinery into the cobalt-blue sky. I turned and made a show of studying the church's arched windows. I loved St. Joseph's Church. During Mass, Father McManus's words soared to the uppermost reaches of the shadowy ceiling and our voices followed. God couldn't help but hear us, and I hoped He noticed my voice louder than the others. I didn't feel slow in church, as the service was always the same. I stood and kneeled and responded without fault, as I had done since a baby. The blue, yellow and red light from the stained-glass saints would wash over me, magically

melting the ever-present knot of anxiety in my stomach.
I shivered and realized how utterly miserable I felt.

"What are you mad at, Rose?" Winnie ran up, two
friends in tow.

"I'm not mad at anything," I told her.

"Well, your face looks mad. Rose tells the best stories," she boasted to her friends. "Tell us one, Rose."

"Not right now, Winnie," I protested weakly. My
head ached so much now, I couldn't keep a single
thought in my mind, let alone an entire story.

"Winnie," I cried. I had just noticed that she only
wore her pinafore and sweater. "Where's your coat?
Mam wouldn't be very pleased to see you outside with
nothing on."

"Oh, Rose. Don't be so fussy."

I felt my back go up at that. I wasn't fussy, was I?

"My coat's too hot. I have two petticoats on, fleece-
lined drawers . . ." Her friends giggled and Winnie
flashed them a naughty grin. "Thick stockings and my
sweater. How could I possibly be cold?"

I couldn't argue with that because I was feeling very
warm myself at the moment.

Without waiting for an answer, she ran away, and
her friends followed. Winnie would always be the
leader, with everyone else hurrying to keep up to her.
She ran to the group of girls around Catherine and
wormed her way into the centre. I tensed, waiting for

Catherine to give her that scornful look of hers, but instead she laughed and patted Winnie's head. I wanted to do that, too. Push right into the group and begin talking like I belonged, but I didn't have Winnie's courage.

The reds, blues and browns of the children's coats blurred in front of my eyes.

"Rose, dear. Are you well?" Sister Therese looked down at me with concern.

I didn't remember sliding down the wall and sitting, but I was on the ground. I scrambled to my feet and staggered slightly when my head swam.

"I do feel a bit strange," I said. I'd never tell Sister Frances I was ill, but Sister Therese was different. She had been my teacher last year and had worked hard to help me with schoolwork. Sister Therese had the sweetest face I had ever seen. ". . . like the Madonna herself," I whispered.

"I beg your pardon?" Sister Therese looked puzzled. She put a hand on my forehead. "You're very hot. Come with me."

I trailed after her into the school and to the teachers' room. I kept my eyes fixed on my scuffed boots, finding the profusion of black habits somewhat overwhelming.

"Sit down here, dear." Sister Therese pushed me into a chair.

Sister Frances cradled a cup of tea in her large hands as she sat at a table talking to the school principal, Sister

Maria Cecilia. She half stood when she saw me, but sat down again as Sister Therese approached them.

"Rose is burning up," Sister Therese said.

"Stuff and nonsense." Sister Frances snorted. "She was fine this morning. She is just playing ill. She is a sly one. She will do anything to get out of her schoolwork."

"I always found Rose to be quiet and biddable. She has some difficulty with her schoolwork, that is true, but she is a good girl and tries—if encouraged," Sister Therese argued. "And it is very difficult to make one's own forehead that hot. She has been outside and it is chilly out there."

I really should polish my boots, I thought.

"Lower your voices." Sister Maria Cecilia swept over and put the back of one hand to my cheek. "She is quite flushed. There is a great deal of influenza going around. She should go home."

Sister Frances loomed behind her, wheezing and blowing annoyance like a steam engine. "Pack up your desk, then, and go home. Take your reader and remember that you have a composition to write. I will expect it to be completed by the time you return."

I nodded quickly and made my escape to the schoolroom. Fearing Sister Frances might sweep in, I tidied my desk at record speed, thrust the reader and a scribbler into my bag, and threw on my coat.

Halfway down the street toward home, I met Ernest and Patrick.

"Why are you out of school? Is it already lunch?" Ernest asked.

"They sent me home early because—" I began.

"Because she's too dumb to learn anything," Patrick finished. He reached into a paper bag he carried, pulled out a sweet and popped it into his mouth.

"Everyone knows she's stupid," Patrick went on. His jaws worked steadily as he chewed.

I felt a hot gush of tears, and caught Patrick's smug smile. He'd seen. I dashed them away and tried to push past. His bulk blocked my way.

"Leave her alone, Patrick," Ernest said suddenly.

"Ah, come on. She's just your dumb sister."

"Leave her alone, I said." Ernest waved a fist under Patrick's nose.

"Fine, then." Patrick backed up a step. "I'm hungry, anyway. I'm going home for dinner. You can walk with your stupid sister."

He lumbered off alone down the hill.

"I don't know how he could be hungry," Ernest said. "He's been eating candy all morning."

I sniffled.

"Aunt Helen gives him bushels of money," he went on.

"Mam says she spoils Patrick something awful because he's her only child. Does he ever share his candy with you?" I asked. I had an envy-green vision of Ernest stuffing his face with peppermint sweets, my particular favourites.

"Patrick? Are you kidding?"

The vision shattered.

"I think Mam and Da should spoil us a little more," Ernest said. "Give us candy."

I managed a weak grin at that.

"Why are you friends with him?" I asked.

"Oh, Patrick's fine most of the time. He's fun. He just teases you because you're slow."

I stared at him.

"Well, you are . . . sort of. I mean, you can't learn anything or read properly." He became defensive.

"I'm not slow," I told him flatly. "It's just . . ."

I didn't really want to talk about this now. I felt weary and talking made my throat raw, but there was something I'd wanted to ask Ernest for the longest time. My fever must be addling my brain, I thought, as I threw all caution to the wind. "Ernest, do the letters in words jump around on you when you're looking at them? Numbers, too?"

"Jump around? What do you mean?"

"Sometimes I look at a word and it's spelled one way, and when I look at it another time, it's spelled differently, as if someone moved the letters around."

"You're nuts, Rose," Ernest said. "Letters jumping around . . ."

I wished I hadn't said anything to him. Was I the only one who had letters move around on her? Was I nuts?

"You look funny. More so than usual. You sick?" Ernest asked.

I nodded. "The principal sent me home."

"I wonder if I could catch it before this afternoon. You think Sister Frances is bad, you should have Brother Simon. He's always cracking his stick across my desk. 'Mr. Dunlea,' he yells. I just about jump out of my skin." Ernest groaned and grabbed his throat. "Sneeze on me, Rose. Make me sick, too."

I knew he was trying to make up for calling me slow and nuts, so I smiled and forgave him. He could make me madder than anyone I know, yet he could also make me laugh the hardest.

We went through the gate and walked to the back of the house and into the kitchen. The sudden warmth enveloped me and I gave a small shudder of pleasure. I didn't ever want to leave here. For a moment I entertained the fantasy of never having to go back to St. Joseph's School. I would stay home and help Mam with the chores. I already could knead bread into a perfect, glistening loaf and Da always praised my currant biscuits. In the afternoon, chores done, Mam and I would sit together and darn Ernest's and Frederick's socks. She said they made holes faster than she could mend them. I swallowed and my sore throat brought my fantasy to an abrupt halt. Da would never let me stay home. He was dead stuck on us all getting an education.

"Rose," Mam exclaimed. She straightened from taking a loaf of bread out of the oven and glanced at the clock beside the cups and saucers on the hutch. "I thought maybe I'd lost track of the time, but you're early."

"I'm not feeling well," I said.

Mam swept over and placed a hand on my forehead. "You're not well, indeed. Upstairs with you and into bed." She looked at Ernest and Bertie and sighed. "I expect you'll just be the first. No doubt everyone will catch it and I'll have a house full of sick people to tend. Go on, now." She gave me a tiny push toward the stairs. "Put on your nightgown. I'll be up in a while with a bit of broth."

I wearily climbed the stairs. My head ached fiercely now and bed sounded good.

"Ernest," Mam said in the kitchen below, "you go to the corner and meet Winnie and walk her the rest of the way home from school."

"Aw, Mam . . ." Ernest protested.

"Do as I say, now, and you can take Bertie with you. It'll keep him from underfoot while I finish with the meal."

I must have slept, because next thing I knew Mam was bent over me, gently shaking my shoulder.

"I have some hot soup for you," she said.

I pushed myself into a sitting position and pulled the blankets about my shoulders against the chill of the bedroom.

"Are you cold?" Mam asked.

I nodded, reached for the spoon and dipped it into

the broth. I enjoyed the trickle of warmth soothing my raw throat.

"I'll get the quilt, then." Mam left the room.

The Irish Chain quilt. Truth is, I would have said I was cold even if it was a heat wave in the middle of July, for a chance to lie under the Irish Chain quilt. It was special, only brought out to drape over the sofa when the priest came to call, or when one of us children was ill. Mam's mother had made it when she was a young woman from patches of material she'd begged and scrounged from her Irish kin. The patches ran diagonally from the top of the quilt to the bottom, looking like links in a chain. And that was what they were—each scrap of material a link to Grandma's home, Ireland, and all those folk gone before her. She'd point to each patch and tell me the story that belonged to it. I never tired of hearing those stories. When she died five years ago, the Irish Chain quilt came to Mam.

Mam returned and spread the quilt over the bed. I burrowed beneath it. Having the quilt over me instantly made me feel better, like being hugged by all the people in the world who loved me. I traced a finger around a feathered swirl of stitching.

"Now you get some rest and stay warm," Mam said. "I think it's just a cold you have, but Mrs. Connelly's twins across the way have diphtheria. I saw the quarantine sign on their door this morning." Her forehead creased. "You've not been over there playing with them, have you?"

"No, Mam. Though Winnie might have."

"I'll check her throat as soon as she's back from the store." She turned to leave the room.

"Mam," I said quickly.

"Yes?"

"Could you tell me a story—from the quilt?"

"Oh, Rose," Mam scolded softly. "I just got Bertie down for a nap and there's ironing to do and the supper to start."

"Please, Mam," I pleaded. "Just a short one."

"You've heard those stories a hundred times," Mam pointed out.

"I know. I like them is all."

Mam rolled her eyes to the ceiling. I knew right then she'd tell me a story.

"Mam," I said. "You're beautiful. Your eyes are like emeralds."

If I had eyes like that, they would go a long way to make up for my red hair. Instead, I had Da's hazel eyes. They could never find one colour to stick with—sometimes grey, sometimes blue, sometimes green.

"Oh, go on with you. And where would you have been seeing emeralds?" Mam laughed but looked pleased. She came and sat on the side of the bed and tucked a stray strand of hair behind my ear. "So it's a story you're flattering me for. Very well, then. Which one?"

I pointed to a faded patch of cream-coloured crepe.

Chapter 3

"That patch—again?" Mam exclaimed.

I nodded. I liked a story from the beginning and, for me, the cream-coloured patch was the beginning.

"My grandmother Rose's wedding dress," Mam said softly. Her fingers briefly caressed it. She sat back to gather her thoughts, then began.

"Great-grandmother Rose lived in Donegal County, in Northern Ireland. The countryside was particularly beautiful that spring in 1833."

"Richly green and lush, filled with birdsong," I added.

Mam raised her eyebrows at me. "Yes, well," she continued, "Rose lived on a small farm—"

"With her Mam and Da and her beloved brother, Danny."

"Perhaps you should be telling the story since you know it so well," Mam said.

"No, you tell it."

"Well, only if you're sure . . ." Mam teased. "Now, where was I? Oh yes, Rose. She was very beautiful—"

"The beauty of the entire county," I interrupted. "Like our Mary."

"Like herself," Mam said emphatically. "Everyone has their own particular beauty. Now, either let me tell the story my way, or I'll leave and you can sleep."

I clamped my mouth shut. This was one threat I knew Mam would keep.

After a moment, she went on. "Most of the land in Ireland at that time was owned by English landlords, who possessed vast estates. They rented out small farms to Irish families. The potato crops were good and the people and the landlords were content.

"Many men courted Rose, some quite prosperous with large holdings, but Rose only had eyes for one—a poor farmer barely eking out an existence on his small tenant farm. He wasn't much to look at, being born with one shoulder higher than the other, and he limped, one leg being shorter than the other. Rose's mother shook her head in despair. 'Why do you want this poor man?' she asked.

"'Because he is kind,' Rose told her. And Rose being Rose went her own way despite all those cautioning her. She visited with the poor man and came to know him and she liked what he was, then she loved what he was. And the poor man, though ugly on the outside, was beautiful on the inside, and though weak on the outside, was strong on the inside, and he had the courage to ask Rose to marry him. And Rose said yes."

Mam tapped me on the nose. "He became your great-grandfather Albert. In the early autumn, Rose and Albert were married, and that is the story of the patch from Rose's wedding dress."

"Now the pink one," I demanded. "The first baby."

"That will be for another day." Mam leaned over and kissed my forehead. "You get some rest. I'll have Winnie or Mary bring you tea later."

I snuggled beneath the quilt. "Mam. Do you remember Great-grandmother Rose?" I asked drowsily.

"Not too well. I was just a little girl when she passed away. I wasn't scared of her like I was some of the other grown-ups. She would scoop me up and set me on her knee and I didn't mind at all. I remember her hands were red and twisted from a life of hard work."

"Why did you name me for her?" I asked.

Mam tilted her head to one side as she thought. "I don't know. I looked at you so tiny in my arms and thought, *this baby's name is Rose.* My grandmother had a lovely smile, very like your own."

"I have a lovely smile?" I asked, surprised.

"Yes, you do and you could use it a bit more. So serious all the time." Mam patted the bed covers in place and left the room.

I closed my eyes, my thoughts drifting. I wished I had known my great-grandmother. My namesake. I also wished I could be like her—able to go my own way. I'd like someone to say that about me. *And Rose being Rose went her own way.* I knew God had made me the way I was, and that was fine, but it would have been nice if

He'd just made me a bit braver and a bit smarter. And if He was going to the trouble to do all that, maybe He could have made me a little bit prettier.

A drawer slammed and brought me up from the depths of a horrible fever dream all mixed up with Sister Frances and Patrick and too many sweets. I opened my eyes to see Mary, dressed in her corset, rapidly opening and shutting drawers in our dresser. She rummaged through the bottom one.

"What are you looking for?" I asked. I sat up and pushed the quilt off me. My nightgown was soaked in sweat.

"Oh, you're awake." Mary walked to the door and shouted downstairs. "Winnie, bring Rose's tea."

She fluffed up the pillow behind my shoulders so I could sit upright. My head throbbed, but—I swallowed tentatively—my throat felt better. Still, I wasn't about to tell Mary or Winnie that because they'd stop being so nice to me.

"I'm looking for my new stockings," Mary explained.

"In a brown parcel?"

"Yes."

"You put them in the chest." I nodded toward a small oak chest standing against the wall beneath the window. It was cedar-lined against moths and held our winter woollens. It also held, pushed deep beneath the clothes, bits and pieces of material of pants and shirts and dresses I'd cut from my family's cast-off, only-good-for-patches-now clothing. Someday, I hoped to make an Irish Chain quilt of my own.

"I remember now," Mary crowed. She rushed over, flipped open the chest lid and pulled her stockings from the brown paper. She ran her fingers over them checking for ladders, then sat on the edge of the bed and pulled one on. "I'm meeting Horace in an hour."

Winnie came in carrying a tray, and we pulled faces at each other behind Mary's back.

"Horace," Winnie said. She plopped the tray down on my lap, spilling tea into the saucer. "That's a dumb name."

"Don't be so silly. A name is a name. That's all." Mary's voice was sharp with annoyance. She wriggled into a dress.

"No," I said. "People suit their names. Ernest is someone who is eager, and our Ernest is definitely that. We call Frederick his full name when he's being forgetful, but Fred when he's working hard on the docks because he's more a man than a boy then . . ."

"What are you going on about?" Mary asked. Dress buttoned, she leaned in toward the mirror and pinched her cheeks to redden them.

"Well, Winnie whines all the time," I went on. "Winnie . . . whine. It suits her."

"I do not," Winnie denied heatedly.

"And you're beautiful like the Virgin Mary who has your name," I told Mary. She didn't know it yet, but I was softening her up for a favour. "And Horace is a . . ." I cast around for a way to describe Horace that wouldn't get me on Mary's bad side. I couldn't find one. ". . . Horace," I finished lamely. I couldn't very well tell her Horace meant a skinny, fussy, vexing man. That reminded me. "I saw Duncan today. He asked after you," I added slyly.

Mary's face flushed slightly.

"I told him you were well and working hard." I hadn't, but I probably would have if I'd thought of it at the time, so it wasn't really a lie.

"You don't need to be talking to Duncan about me," Mary said.

She ran her hands down her dress, smoothing the skirt.

"Well, he asked. It would be rude if I didn't answer. He's very handsome," I added.

"I wouldn't know." Mary grabbed up her coat and shrugged it on. "He's just Duncan. So does he suit his name? Does Duncan mean a milk delivery boy?"

"And what is wrong with Duncan delivering milk?" Mam stood in the doorway, frowning at Mary.

"Nothing." Mary rooted around in her pockets avoiding Mam's gaze. "Just a silly game Rose was playing, about people suiting their names."

"Duncan is a hard-working boy. He's learning his

father's dairy business from the bottom up so he'll know it through and through when he takes over."

"I know that, Mam. It just means he'll never leave *here*." Mary spread her arms wide, embracing our room, but I knew she meant the north part of Halifax— Richmond, where we lived.

Mary told me once in secret that she felt suffocated, by our house, the family, the neighbourhood. Her only escape was the bank. I'd only been downtown once, when Mary treated me to an afternoon in a tea room. The white linen and polished knives and forks had made me so anxious I'd upset my teacup. I'd been happy to get back home where I felt safe.

Winnie and I held our breaths, waiting for Mam's explosion. Mam didn't get mad easily but when she did, we all cleared out of her way—fast. Even Mary looked wary now, but also determined.

"Some of us have happy lives *here*," Mam said mildly. "Your Da and me."

Mary opened her mouth, but Mam stopped her before she spoke. "Happiness doesn't come from things you own or the place you live, but from inside you. Some people search far and wide for happiness all their lives, when all the time it was right under their nose. There's nothing wrong with venturing out into the world, but don't deny your home."

Mary shook her head defiantly. "I know what I want, Mam."

"Do you? Where are you off to, then?"

"Horace is taking me to a play," Mary said. "I'm meeting him downtown."

"Most young men come calling for their young women. They don't meet them downtown."

"That was in the olden days, Mam. Things are different now."

"We're having the family and a few friends in Saturday night. It would be nice if Horace could come," Mam said calmly.

"It's a long way for him to travel . . ." Mary began.

"I'm sure he'll be happy to come if you ask him, and he does have his motor car."

And that was the end of that, though the air remained thick with unsaid words—words of Mary's discontent, restlessness and wanting; Mam's anger and hurt. I fancied I could see Mary impatiently pushing them aside as she made her way out of the room.

Mam strode over to the bed and felt my forehead. "You're cooler now. Winnie, you'll sleep with Mary tonight so Rose can have a good rest."

Winnie and I usually shared a bed, and I looked forward to the unaccustomed luxury of not having her limbs wrapped around me all night long. There were definite benefits to being sick. Mam left the room, taking the empty tray with her. I didn't remember eating the bread or drinking the tea, but I must have. I suddenly grimaced. I'd forgotten to ask Mary for my favour.

"Do you hurt somewhere?" Winnie asked. She threw herself down on Mary's bed.

"No, just remembered something I forgot," I replied.

"That doesn't make sense. If you remembered it, then it's not forgot," she pointed out.

"Never mind, Winnie." The way she figured things out tied my brain up in knots.

"Why did you tell Mam I'd been visiting the twins?" she demanded.

"I thought you had," I told her.

"Well, I had been, but you didn't need to tell her. She swabbed my throat out."

"She doesn't want you getting their sickness."

"I never get sick," Winnie announced. "Though I should," she added thoughtfully. "You get your tea in bed, everyone being nice to you. And you get to have the Irish Chain quilt. I could pretend I'm sick."

"Mam would know and she'd swab your throat twice as much."

"Yes, she probably would," Winnie admitted.

"Martha Schultz was asking after you," Winnie said after a moment.

"I bet." I sniffed.

"She was," Winnie insisted. "She said she might drop by tomorrow and see how you were."

"She could have asked me at school today," I pointed out.

"No, she couldn't. She had to be with her Catherine and her friends."

My eyes felt hot with unshed tears. "But *I'm* her friend, too. Or I was."

"That was before you failed your grades. She can't very well be friends with you at school now because then no one would talk to her. And there's no point in both of you not being talked to." Winnie's skirt flew over her head as she jumped on Mary's bed. I eyed her bouncing body enviously. The world was so black and white for her. She accepted everything the way it was. Maybe that was the secret to happiness.

Bertie came into the room, thumb in his mouth, and crawled under the quilt beside me.

Winnie bounced from Mary's bed to mine and settled at the end. "Tell a story, Rose. You tell the best stories. I almost feel like they're real."

I knew she was buttering me up, but so seldom did anyone say I did anything the best that I felt a small glow.

"But stories are for bedtime," I teased them. It was my job to tell Bertie a story each night before bed. It was the only way Mam could get him to go quietly.

"We *are* in bed," Bertie said.

I hugged him. "You're right. We are in bed. Though I don't know how pleased Mam would be to find you here next to me with my cold." But I didn't push him away. The company felt nice.

"How about the story of Great-grandmother Rose's baby?" I asked. I did like my stories running in order, and Mam wouldn't have time to tell it.

"Oh, Rose. Why do you always want to tell those stories from the quilt?" Winnie complained. "I've heard them a hundred times from Mam and you. Tell me the one about the princess on Citadel Hill."

I had made up a story for Winnie and Bertie about a princess held captive in the Citadel above Halifax waiting for a prince, who somewhat resembled Duncan, to rescue her. Today I wanted the story from the quilt.

"About the baby or nothing. I am sick," I reminded her.

Winnie sighed, then settled down. She would hear about the baby.

"Rose and Albert were married and lived in a small stone cottage with a thatched roof."

"What's a thatched roof?" Winnie asked.

"It's a roof made of grass," I told her.

"Green growing grass? Did their goats graze up there?" Winnie was intrigued.

"No, it's a thick, dried grass, bundled and tied together to make a roof," I said. "You've asked me all this before, so stop interrupting." I took a deep breath and continued.

"The cottage was cosy with red roses growing up the

outside walls, and Rose made it a lovely home. A year later their first baby was born. They called him Albert after his father. He was a perfect baby with soft, pink skin and a sunny smile. Rose and Albert loved him dearly. They carried him to church in a beautiful christening gown that Rose had made"—I stroked the faded pink square—"and had him baptized. Baby Albert was so good he didn't make one single peep when the priest held him. But one morning Rose went in to get Baby Albert and he was lying still and cold in his cradle." I lowered my voice. "With a moan, Rose gathered the tiny babe in her arms. She tried to wake him, but his eyes would not open. Rose's tears fell upon his face. 'We loved him too much,' she cried to her husband. 'No,' Albert replied. 'God loved him even more than we did, and wanted our baby to be with Him. You can't love a child too much.' And right before their eyes Baby Albert sprouted white wings and flew up to Heaven."

"That's a fib," Winnie announced. "Babies don't grow wings."

"It's not a fib. It's a story," I told her. "And he became an angel so he would have wings."

"Well, Rose and Albert had six more children," Winnie said practically. "Including our granny, and it's a good thing she didn't die as a baby or we wouldn't be born." She threw off the quilt. "I smell supper."

She raced out of the room and downstairs.

"Did I have wings when I was a baby?" asked Bertie.

"No, you're an alive boy, not an angel," I said. I heard the back door open, then the voices of Da and Fred fill the kitchen. I gently pushed Bertie from the bed. "Da's home. Go down to supper."

I listened contentedly to the family sounds in the kitchen, and gently fingered the pale pink patch. Six more children or not, Great-grandmother Rose would never forget that first child and neither had my grandma. She'd put his christening gown in the quilt.

I studied the other patches, silently repeating to myself whom they belonged to and the stories tied to each. Winnie's question came back to me. Why did I always want to tell the stories of the quilt? I'd not really thought about that before, but now that I did, I realized it was because of a belief I had. I believed there was a key somewhere inside the Irish Chain quilt—a key to how to be brave and strong like Great-grandmother Rose. And if I kept telling the stories, maybe someday I might find it.

Chapter 4

After two days in bed, on Saturday morning Mam declared me well enough to get up. The house was quiet. Winnie had gone to a friend's to play, and Ernest had taken Bertie to see the cadets on parade at Wellington Barracks. Da and Fred were putting in extra time at the docks, while Mary enjoyed her Saturday morning lie-in. I felt a deep contentment being alone with Mam as we sat and darned socks.

"It's never-ending, Rose," Mam said. She sighed and waggled her fingers through a hole in the heel of Fred's sock. "I'm now darning my darning."

I liked when Mam spoke to me as if I were a grown-up. Suddenly, I desperately wanted it to be this way always. "Mam. Why can't I stay home with you instead of going back to school? I hate it there. I could do all the darning. I'd be a big help," I pleaded.

"Rose, dear . . ." Mam began.

"Please, Mam? I could keep everything mended. You know I do a good job."

"You are very good with a needle, Rose. Better than me, but—"

A knock at the kitchen door silenced Mam. A shrill voice called, "Hello? Anyone home?"

Aunt Helen.

Mam rolled her eyes heavenward. I could have stamped my feet I was so mad at Aunt Helen for interrupting. Now I'd have to start to talk to Mam all over again. It wasn't easy to get her to myself.

"Rose, would you put this sewing in my room, please. And then I think it's time Mary got up, if you'd go wake her." Mam held out the socks and wool, then picked up a pair of Ernest's pants and handed them to me, too. "These can go in my patch bag. That's all they're good for now."

Aunt Helen sailed into the room. "I was just at the store and thought I'd drop in on my way back and see if there is anything you need for this evening."

"I think we have—" Mam began.

"You know, you have to be awful careful in the shops these days. I tell you, I saw the clerk put a finger on the scale when he weighed the sugar. Have you noticed that lately?"

"No, I—" Mam said.

"Well, I told him to just take those fingers off. He gave me quite a look, but you can't pull the wool over my eyes. You'd think with the war and prices so high— why would they need to lean on the scale to cheat a person?" Aunt Helen raised her eyebrows.

"I really wouldn't—"

"Greed. That's why. Would there be a spot of tea left in the pot?"

There wasn't anything in the pot, but Mam couldn't get a word in edgewise to tell Aunt Helen so. I caught sight of Mary on the stairs, grinning widely, and had to lower my head to hide my smile.

Aunt Helen took a deep breath, preparing for her next gush of words. I watched, fascinated, as her large bosom heaved up and down. That woman could proudly adorn the prow of a ship, I'd overheard Da tell Mam once. Mam had laughed and quickly shushed him.

It must be hard, though, I thought, for Aunt Helen to catch her breath with her stout figure laced tightly into a corset. Too bad her tongue wasn't tied in, too.

"And how are you, Rose?"

I didn't bother to answer.

"Patrick said you were under the weather with the influenza. Concerned about you, he was. He's such a thoughtful, caring boy."

Caring? Patrick with his cutting words and hurtful pranks?

"But missing time from school, Rose. What a shame. You can't afford that, can you? You don't want to be held back yet again."

"Helen." Mam's voice was sharp. She'd caught my stricken look. "Come into the kitchen for tea."

"Now, Rose will be thirteen come this next April . . ."

"Fourteen," I yelled in my frustration.

Aunt Helen gasped and placed a gloved hand on her chest. "There is no need to shout." With a backward look at me, she followed Mam into the kitchen. "Really! Young people and their manners these days. What was I saying? Oh yes. She could leave school at the end of this year. Even with her simple ways, I'm sure you could get her into service. Perhaps as a laundry maid."

I went slowly into Mam's room and set the darning on a chair, then lowered myself to the bed. *Simple ways. Get her into service!* I'd never thought that if I left school I'd have to go to work. I thought I'd stay here, safe with Mam and Da. I didn't want to be in a stranger's house trying to follow their orders. I'd get things mixed up and they'd be mad at me. School or a stranger's house. Some choice.

I unfolded Ernest's old pants and shook them out, then searched in Mam's sewing box for her scissors. I cut a small square of material and put it in my pocket. On my hands and knees, I fumbled under Mam's bed and pulled out the patch bag. It held all the clothes we'd outgrown or worn to pieces. Mam used the leftover material to mend holes on knees and elbows. I dumped the bag out to see if anything new had been added since I'd last seen it, and pulled out a flowered skirt. It had been Mary's, then mine, and Winnie had worn it this past summer but had outgrown it come autumn. I cut a couple of squares from it and tucked them in my pocket with the other.

I went back out and heard Aunt Helen, and escaped up the stairs to the bedroom. Mary stood in front of the mirror running a comb through her hair. She held my eyes with her mirrored ones.

"She is without a doubt the most terrible woman," she said.

I shrugged. Aunt Helen had been around forever, so I was pretty used to her ways.

"I'll have to keep Horace away from her tonight. What he'll think, I don't know. And Grandpa. If he does that thing where he takes out his teeth and chases the young ones with them, I'll just die." Mary sighed and laid down her brush.

"Doesn't Horace have a grandpa, too?" I asked.

"I imagine so," Mary answered impatiently. "But not all grandfathers go pulling out their teeth at parties. At least, not those from the south side of town!"

The south side of town. That is where the rich people live. That is where the girls from here went to go into service. I felt like a fist had plowed into my stomach. That is where I would have to go to be a laundry maid.

I went over to the chest and raised the lid. From beneath the woollens, I pulled out my bits 'n' pieces bag, opened it and dropped in the patches. The bag was quite heavy now, I realized as I tucked it away again.

But then, it contained two years' worth of collected bits of material. I had scraps of Da's and Frederick's work shirts, a patch from an apron of Granny Dunlea's that she'd set afire one day when she bent too close to the stove. She said she often felt as if her stomach was burning inside, but that was the first time she'd ever seen actual flames. I also had a sleeve from a blouse of my other grandma, Mam's mother, and a patch cut from a corner of Bertie's old nightgown. I closed the lid of the chest.

Mary pulled out two dresses, looked them over, sighed and hung them back on the hook near her bed. "Horace has seen me in both of these. I need something different." She unfolded a skirt and a waist and held them to her chest while she studied herself in the mirror.

"That looks nice," I offered.

Mary frowned and tossed them on the bed. "The skirt will never do. It's flannel. I look dowdy. Horace's sister came into the bank the other day and you should have seen the beautiful blue wool skirt she had on, and a smart jacket to match. And their house, Rose—Horace took me there one day when the family was out. It was so grand. A porch right across the entire front of the house and two bay windows. Inside, the floors gleam and there's a morning room . . ."

A room where you only sat in the morning seemed a terrible waste of space to me, but I listened politely.

". . . and a parlour with a marble fireplace. Over the dining-room table, a chandelier that shines like diamonds. It made me dizzy just to see, and a library full of books." Mary's face shone with her enthusiasm.

I had closed my eyes to better picture the house as she described it, but they flew open at the word *books*. I never had asked Mary for that favour. I concentrated hard to keep the thought in my mind so it wouldn't slip out again.

"I peeked into his sister's bedroom," Mary went on. "Her wardrobe door was open and the wardrobe jammed with clothes. Imagine having so many clothes no one would see me in the same outfit twice in one month. Oh, Rose. I'd love to live in a house like that— have a life like that."

"Do they have maids?" I asked suddenly.

"I imagine so," Mary said. "His mother wouldn't do the work herself. Not polishing all those floors."

"Mam does."

"Their house is much bigger than ours, and besides, his mother is a lady."

Surely, Mam was a lady, too.

Mary caught my look. "I mean, Mam's respectable, but his mother's a society lady," she explained. "Oh, never mind. Yes, they have maids and a cook."

"Aunt Helen says I should go into service," I said. "I don't want to live in a big house."

"Well, maybe someday if I live in a grand house like

that, you could come and work for me. We wouldn't tell anyone you were my sister, of course."

"Why not?"

"Because I couldn't very well be a society lady with a maid for a sister, could I?"

I didn't quite know why, but I nodded my head to keep her happy. In the meantime, a horrible thought occurred to me.

"Does that mean you are going to marry Horace?"

Mary flushed and began to brush down her flannel skirt. "Well, he's not asked me. But he does seem to like me. He is coming tonight, after all. Oh, Rose, you have to help me keep him away from Aunt Helen and Grandpa. They could ruin my chances."

Her chances for the big house, the maids, the clothes, the books in the library.

"Mary. Could you read me my homework?"

"Not now, Rose. Just read it yourself. I can't always be here to help you with your lessons."

"Please, Mary."

She must have heard the plea in my voice. "Tomorrow, Rose. I promise. Now leave me alone so I can find an outfit to wear tonight."

I watched her for a few minutes. Something she had said pricked at my mind. I concentrated hard like I'd trained myself to, and it came to me. "Mary. Why did Horace take you to see his house when his family was away?"

Mary shrugged, uninterested, and held up a sweater to her chin. "Maybe they just happened to all be out."

I wandered down the stairs. I didn't understand Mary. I loved our house on Albert Street. It was small, but we fit cosily. Our street was cinders and the out-houses smelled something awful in summer, but I liked the way the buildings crowded together, some leaning wearily against a neighbour, as if they were helping each other out just like the people here did. I never wanted to leave it, or Mam or Da, yet Mary, she was raring to go. I sat on the stairs. I've asked God before why He made us all so different, but He hasn't answered yet. It unset-tled me to think Mary might leave and become a society lady, but no matter how much I wanted it, I couldn't make her stay. If only she liked Duncan instead of Horace. Duncan would make Mary stay.

Aunt Helen's voice floated up the stairs from the kitchen. ". . . she has the kidney complaint, you know."

I tiptoed into the parlour to avoid the kidney com-plaint or the liver complaint or any other complaint. Now it was me feeling restless and cooped up. I looked out the window and felt the tug of wind and cloud-tossed skies. Mam wouldn't be happy if I went out with my cold still lingering, but I grabbed my coat anyway and quietly let myself out the front door.

There is something about wind reddening the cheeks and ears that makes a person feel extra alive. I put my arms out and let a violent gust blow my coat out behind me. Like a kite, I thought. I dipped and whirled, remembering the wildly dancing kite Frederick had made for Ernest, Winnie and me. Or rather, made for us, but flown himself. *You'd break it*, he told us, but I think he liked making it soar near the clouds. *Soar*. I repeated the word to myself. It held a magic, one that could carry a person on and on. *Soar*. Could I reach Heaven? Could people visit God and then come back?

"What are you doing?"

I fell back to earth with a resounding *clunk* to find Patrick in front of me. I'd not seen him come up.

"The wind blew my coat and I was trying to close it," I hastily fibbed. More for the confessional. The first Thursday of every month I arrived at church with my long list of sins and left with my equally long penance of Hail Marys and Our Fathers.

Patrick fished around in a small brown bag, drew his hand out and popped a red candy into his mouth. He held out the bag to me. Surprised, I reached forward, only to have the bag pulled away when I touched the paper top. He laughed hugely, his tongue, red from the sweet, bright against his pale, doughy face. I imagined myself kneading that dough, reforming his features with my fists. I must have stared for a while because he shifted the bag to his other hand then back again.

"What are you looking at?" he asked finally.

I didn't say anything. My silence made him uneasy. Had I found an unexpected way to get back at Patrick?

He took a couple of steps backward. "You're crazy. You know that? You're not just simple, but crazy. They'll lock you up at the lunatic asylum if you go around staring at people like that."

Thoughts scrambled rapidly through my mind— *answer him? Punch him? Cry? Run? Lunatic.* I stood mute.

He threw the empty bag at me, but the wind caught it and sent it sailing back at him. He swatted it away angrily. "Crazy Rose." He started down the hill.

"He's not very nice, is he."

I whirled about to find Martha Schultz behind me. She, too, had a wary look in her eyes. I wondered if she thought I was crazy, but her next words revealed her discomfort.

"I'm sorry I don't talk to you at school anymore," she said. She clipped her words short, her German accent more pronounced when she was nervous. She and her family had lived in Halifax for five years. Her father ran a bakery and she always smelled faintly of yeast and cinnamon. "It's just, you're held back and Catherine . . ." She stopped. "Please say you're not mad, Rose. Can't we be friends outside of school? Catherine isn't half as nice as you."

I looked at my feet, and then up at the sky. I couldn't stop the hurt feeling, but I missed Martha. I needed her to be my friend, and if it had to be outside of school, I guess I could live with that. Besides, as Mam said,

Martha did have a big heart and it wasn't her fault she didn't have any gumption. That was how God had made her.

"Do you want to walk up to the park?" I asked.

She smiled, relieved. "As long as you feel well enough. Winnie said you had a dreadful cold. In fact, I'm surprised to see you out today. She made it sound like you were seriously ill."

I laughed. "Winnie would. She exaggerates everything. She likes being the centre of attention." Whereas I didn't want to be noticed—or did I? Maybe that was just something I'd told myself so many times I believed it.

"I brought you some pastries from the bakery," Martha said. "They have jam in them."

My appetite returned all of a sudden.

We walked up the hill toward the park, leaning into the wind. "Why do the girls at school do what Catherine wants?" I asked as I bit into a pastry. It melted in my mouth in a heavenly mixture of dough and jam.

Martha shrugged. "I don't know. We just do."

"But she's not even from around here," I protested. "At least I was born in Richmond. And she's not Catholic and I am."

"Well, I guess because you've been held back, Rose. We talk about stuff in our class and you wouldn't know anything about that."

"But some girls have been held back because they've been ill and Catherine still speaks to them," I pointed out.

"But you haven't been ill," Martha said.

We could talk about this all afternoon but the fact was Catherine had her mind set against me and nothing I could do would change that. I popped the last bit of pastry into my mouth.

"Unfasten your coat," I said. "Let it hang loose. The wind is so strong it nearly raises you off your feet. You feel like a kite."

Martha undid her coat, and a moment later, we were laughing wildly.

Chapter 5

Da, Fred, Uncle Lyle and Grandpa huddled on the
back porch, white smoke curling about their heads.
Mam had thrown a surprised look when Fred had
joined them and lighted a cigarette, but Da had merely
said "He works a man's job," and Mam had turned
away. Gusts of male laughter drifted into the kitchen,
narrowing Aunt Helen's and Granny's lips into thin
lines of disapproval. Winnie and I arranged sandwiches
on plates while Mam set out a large pot of tea.

The back door blew open and Aunt Ida swept in,
face rosy.

"Still got the honeymoon blooms in her cheeks,"
Aunt Helen said to Mam.

Aunt Ida flushed a deeper red. "It's the cold," she
protested.

I liked Aunt Ida. Tiny and pretty with curly black
hair and sapphire blue eyes, she had what Mam called a
sensible manner. She had run a spinning machine in the
Dominion Textile factory until she married Uncle
James and he had insisted his wife stay home and keep
house. They lived two streets up the hill from us in
rented rooms. Uncle James worked with Da on the

docks, and they looked so much alike dressed in their work clothes and caps that sometimes I had to look twice to see who was who.

Aunt Ida held out a plate of shortbread. No one came to a party empty-handed. "I left James out there with the men. Smoking," she added.

"Foul habit," Granny muttered. She shuffled about the kitchen, scrawny, head bobbing. She looked for all the world like one of her own chickens. I stifled a giggle and stored that thought away to tell Winnie later.

"Let them enjoy themselves," Mam said. "They all work so hard these days. Besides, we should be grateful we have men on the porch to smoke. Many women these days are all alone, widowed or their men at war."

Aunt Ida's honeymoon blooms paled.

"What's the matter, dear?" Mam asked.

Aunt Ida looked around the room, then said softly, "It's James. He talks about the war all the time. I'm terrified he'll join up. I don't want him to go over there. So many men don't return." Her knuckles whitened as she gripped the ladder-back of a chair.

"He's doing war work down on the docks," Mam said soothingly.

"I tell him that, but he wants to be over there. 'In the thick of things,' he says." Aunt Ida looked ready to burst into tears.

"Well, it's a woman's lot to stay at home and wait for the men to return from war," Aunt Helen said.

"There's nothing you can do or say if he has his mind set on it."

"Well, if women did say something, maybe there wouldn't be a war," Aunt Ida retorted. Her cheeks reddened again, but this time with indignation.

"Have you been going to those political rallies?" Aunt Helen asked suspiciously. "The vote for women." She sniffed.

"You can bet your buttons women would not vote for a war," Aunt Ida argued.

"You better not bring any of those suffragette ideas into this house," Aunt Helen told her.

"Whose house?" Mam inquired.

"Could Michael speak to him?" Aunt Ida turned to Mam.

"I'll ask him, but I'm afraid I have to agree with Helen," Mam said with a certain amount of reluctance. No one liked to admit they sided with Aunt Helen. "Once a man's mind is made up, it's hard to change." She clapped her hands suddenly. "But why are we all standing around with long, gloomy faces? Maybe the war will be over soon and there will be nothing for James to go to."

"You better pray for the war to end with your Fred getting older," Granny said.

This time it was Mam's cheeks that paled.

Neighbours began to arrive and the house filled up. I found a spot halfway up the staircase. From here, I had long ago discovered, I could see most of the kitchen and parlour, yet few people noticed me. I liked a party, the food, the music and singing, the laughter. Liked it, that is, if left to myself.

Patrick and Ernest came in, and I shrank into the shadows of the staircase so they wouldn't see me. Winnie flitted from one knot of people to another, enjoying the pats on her head and pinches on her cheeks. She was also, I saw, accumulating a fair number of sweets. As usual, Aunt Helen's voice rang out over everyone else's.

"Poor Mrs. Harold Jones," Aunt Helen announced. "The cancer growing in her, they say. She won't live long." Her tone might have been sombre, but her eyes shone bright with the news she brought.

"Once you get the cancer, you don't live long." Granny shook her head, but I knew she enjoyed the gossip as much as Aunt Helen.

I had a sudden vision of the two of them at Granny's kitchen table, tongues wagging over the symptoms and dire consequences of all The Illnesses, washed down with endless cups of tea.

The back door banged and the men came in from the porch. A heady mixture of fresh air and smoke swept in with them. At some point Duncan must have arrived, for he followed Frederick into the room. He gave a quick glance around—looking for Mary, I realized—but she and Horace had gone for an early supper and had not returned.

Our seldom-used front door opened and Father McManus came in. Mam rushed up, took his flat black hat and ushered him in. Voices quieted as heads nodded greetings to the priest, then picked up again as he passed into the parlour. Mam and Aunt Helen exchanged a pleased glance. It was a point of honour among the women at St. Joseph's for one of the priests to put in an appearance at their parties. Da and the other men appeared less pleased. They'd have to guard their tongues with Father in the house.

I settled back on the step. If it was such an honour to have a priest at a party, I wondered as I watched Mam fuss and bring Father a cup of tea, what would the women say if God came? Imagine how surprised Mam would be if I turned up at the party with God, a white, shining presence, in tow. Aunt Helen would be speechless as she watched Him bite into a sandwich. I smiled at the thought of a silenced Aunt Helen. Perhaps He'd wrap an arm around Da's shoulder, tell a joke from the old country, Heaven, and burst into song, though it would be a hymn, with Him being God and all. I swallowed a giggle and offered up a quick apology in case I had offended Him in any way.

Grandpa, I saw, had his false teeth out and was chasing Bertie and Winnie around the kitchen. I remembered the delicious fright of those clacking teeth. Mr. Neeson from down the street had brought his fiddle. He drew the bow across the strings, adding to the general bedlam. At that moment the front door opened again and Mary came in with Horace. She took one look at the chaos and froze. Suddenly, a huge smile appeared on her face, but even from my spot on the stairs I could see it didn't reach her eyes. She took Horace's coat to reveal a suit and collar. He was the only man in the room other than Father McManus to be dressed in clothes that weren't work shirts, suspenders and coarse twill pants. Perhaps Horace had to wear his suit all the time because he was a banker, the way Father McManus always wore a collar and cassock because he was a priest.

Mary steered Horace quickly past Aunt Helen, took one look at toothless Grandpa and pushed Horace into the kitchen. I slid my bottom down two steps and strained my neck around the wall to watch their progress.

Mam held her hand out to Horace. I felt proud of her, looking so beautiful with her cheeks flushed from heat. Wispy strands of hair escaped her knot to frame her face. I don't believe any society lady could look better. Da, his sleeves rolled up to show his combinations at the wrists, briefly shook Horace's hand. Suddenly Grandpa came up, slipped his teeth in and pumped Horace's hand up and down. I quickly stood and pushed through the people, anxious to hear whatever Grandpa had to say.

"Horse, you say?" Grandpa put a hand behind his ear. I was surprised as I'd not known his hearing was going. "Horse? Funny sort of name for your folks to give you."

Duncan and Fred snickered behind their hands, though I noticed Duncan's eyes did not leave Mary's face—hadn't, in fact, since she'd entered the room.

"Grandfather." Mary's eyes shot daggers at all of them. "His name is *Hor-ace!* Horace!" She turned to Horace, and I swear I could hear her teeth grind. "Please don't mind my grandfather, he has recently become hard of hearing."

Very recently.

"Mother," she said. "Do you need any help?"

Mother! Mam levelled a look at her. "I think we're just fine, thank you, daughter."

Mam's voice was sweet, but I could tell she was vexed something terrible with Mary. Mary knew it, too. She looked around desperately.

"Oh, Horace, this is Father McManus from St. Joseph's Church." She led Horace into the parlour and over to the priest. Again I followed. Father McManus looked mildly surprised to find Mary and Horace suddenly materialize in front of him but shook hands willingly.

"So, you're not from around these parts," he said.

"No." Horace swept the room with small, black eyes. His fingers fiddled with his cuffs. "No. I live on the south side."

The room stilled as he spoke. Even Aunt Helen stopped her chatter to hear Mary's beau.

"Horace's father is the manager of the bank I work at," Mary said. "And Horace works there, too. He'll take over from his father someday," she added proudly.

"Oh, well, that's not definite." Horace gave a dry laugh. It was obviously definite in his mind.

"So what church are you with?" Father McManus asked heartily.

You could have heard a pin drop, the room was so quiet.

"Anglican," Horace answered. He darted a quick glance around the room, now aware of the silence, the faces turned toward him, bodies still as statues. "Anglican," he repeated.

Could silence change its character? At first it had been expectant, now it had a definite shocked feeling. Aunt Helen and Granny exchanged meaningful glances. Imagine—an Anglican in the middle of a room full of Catholics.

Mam's mouth stretched in a horrified O, and she stared at Horace as if he had committed a mortal sin.

"Lovely cathedral you have there," Father McManus said, not the least bit concerned that he was talking to an Anglican.

Mary suddenly grabbed a plate of sandwiches and thrust them toward Horace. "Refreshment, Horace? Father? Horace drives a Roadster, Father," she said, anxious to steer the talk away from religion.

"A Roadster. Well, imagine that." Father seemed at a loss for anything further to say.

Mary held out the sandwich plate again and the two men each took one. Horace pulled a handkerchief from a pocket and dabbed at his hands after each bite. As there was nothing left to hear, conversation started up again.

"Anglican!" Aunt Helen exclaimed loudly to Aunt Ida. "Whatever is Mary thinking? This is what comes of people getting above their station in life. If Mary had stayed here and worked in the factory like the rest of our girls, well, she wouldn't be so uppity."

"I think it's wonderful that Mary has a job typewriting," Aunt Ida announced. "She's done very well for herself."

Aunt Ida was fast becoming my favourite aunt.

I went back to my seat on the stairs. Winnie joined me with a plate of sandwiches and cookies to share. I absently bit into a meat sandwich, my ears still tuned to the conversation between my two aunts.

Aunt Helen shook her head. "God gives each and every person a rightful place. You try to go against His wishes and this is what happens. You get Anglicans. Aren't I right, Father?"

Father McManus turned, a second sandwich halfway to his mouth. "Yes, indeed," he said. I knew he had no idea what he was agreeing to, but most people did anything to not carry on a conversation with Aunt Helen.

Aunt Helen was enormously satisfied. She puffed up her chest and preened like one of Granny's hens about to lay. "See, even Father agrees with me."

Winnie and I giggled.

"Grown-ups are so funny," Winnie said.

I nodded.

"Did you know *Horse* wasn't Catholic?" she asked.

Poor Horace. He'd be known as *Horse* in our family forever now.

I shook my head, my mouth full of chopped ham and bread.

Aunt Helen was still revelling in Father McManus's agreement. "Well, at least Michael and Alice won't have the same problem with Rose. That girl hasn't the brains to go above her station."

I set down my sandwich, appetite gone.

"And grown-ups can be horrid," Winnie whispered. "And Aunt Helen is the horridest."

"You shouldn't say things like that about your elders," I scolded half-heartedly.

"Why not? They say things like that about us," Winnie pointed out. I couldn't argue with that.

Patrick loomed in front of me. "This is how Rose reads . . ." Cookie crumbs flew from his overstuffed mouth as he spoke. "I . . . I . . . can . . . can . . . can't . . . re . . . re . . ."

From over Patrick's shoulder, I saw Mam's face flush red with anger. She pushed through the party-goers toward us with *Patrick is going to get a talking to* written all over her face. Da noticed, too, and tried to follow, but he wasn't going to reach Mam in time to stop her. He knew life wouldn't be worth living if there was a breach between Aunt Helen and Mam. Suddenly, Aunt Ida was there.

"That's very mean, Patrick," Aunt Ida said.

"Yes," Aunt Helen blustered. She wasn't happy that Aunt Ida had chided Patrick instead of her, especially in front of their friends. "That was very mean," she went on loudly. "You should be kind to the unfortunates." She nodded her head, pleased to have done her job as a mother.

Unfortunates! She made me sound like one of the people in the lunatic asylum. I wanted to crawl away. Mam had reached us now, looking as if she was going to burst she was so mad.

"Rose is a lovely girl," Aunt Ida went on. She put a hand on Mam's shoulder to calm her. "And an excellent storyteller. In fact, why don't you tell one of your stories now, Rose. I enjoy them so very much."

I was struck dumb. Tell a story? In front of all these people? I looked at Mam in silent appeal, but she shrugged helplessly. Aunt Ida took my hand and led me to the middle of the parlour. *Please, God, open the floor and let it swallow me. Please, God.* Nothing happened. He must be busy elsewhere—but what could be more important than this!? I was about to disgrace myself in front of the entire neighbourhood. Everyone sat expectant, smiles plastered on their faces. I knew what they thought: poor, *unfortunate* Rose. Aunt Ida nodded encouragingly, so I took a deep breath and thought of the coarse blue patch in the Irish Chain quilt.

"This is . . . this is the story of—from my . . . my great-grandmother Rose's life," I croaked.

"A little louder, dear. Let everyone hear you," Aunt Ida said.

"From . . . from Mam's Irish Chain quilt. I mean, it's a story from a patch—It's made of patches. Rose and Albert lived . . . they lived . . ." My brain fizzled and died. I couldn't remember where they lived. I looked at the faces turned toward me. Two stood out: Patrick's, gloating, and Duncan's, sympathetic. I cringed. I'd take Patrick's over Duncan's any day. I was an *unfortunate.*

"Rose has been ill with a cold," Mam said. She came up and put a hand on my forehead. "In fact, you're quite warm again. I think you should go up to bed."

Mam, not God, gave me a way to leave the room. *Where were You when I needed You?* I thought angrily, then immediately apologized. After all, perhaps God had told Mam to say that. I mustn't vex Him. Tears blurred my eyes as I stumbled up the stairs.

"It could be the scarlet fever," Aunt Helen said. "It affects the brain."

I turned and looked back to see Mary bundle Horace into his coat and hurry him out the door. I don't think anyone else noticed—no one except Duncan. Face desolate, he watched them go.

"I heard the O'Reillys lost their two youngest to the scarlet fever just last week," Granny said. "Or was it the whooping cough."

As I reached the top of the stairs, Mr. Neeson drew his bow across his fiddle, then Da's voice filled the room as he sang:

> *My wild Irish Rose,*
> *the sweetest flower that grows.*
> *You may search everywhere*
> *but none can compare*
> *with my wild Irish Rose.*

Chapter 6

I felt the bed shift beneath me and pried open heavy eyes to see Aunt Ida perched on the edge, a troubled expression on her face.

"I'm sorry, Rose," she said. "I shouldn't have made you stand in front of everyone. I was just so mad at Patrick for making fun of you. I didn't think."

I struggled to sit up, and Aunt Ida quickly put a pillow behind my back. I pulled the Irish Chain quilt up to my chin, then pleated it with my fingers, glad Mam hadn't put it away yet. I needed its comfort.

"I enjoy hearing about your great-grandmother. I have no family left of my own so I've sort of adopted yours. In fact, I wouldn't mind hearing a story about them right now." She smiled, looking so sweet that I could see why Uncle James was smitten with her. I was, too.

I pointed to a rough woollen blue patch in the quilt. "I was going to tell them about this one," I said. "It's from my great-grandpa Albert's work pants."

Aunt Ida settled herself to listen, lips parted in anticipation.

"Rose and Albert lived in Northern Ireland," I said. I was surprised the words came so easily. Telling a story to Aunt Ida was like telling one to Winnie.

"They were very happy on the small farm with their six children. It might have been rented land, but Albert treated it with loving care. Like all the other farmers, he planted potatoes every year.

"'Why do we plant nothing but potatoes?' Rose asked one spring.

"'It's what grows best here,' Albert told her.

"'Would it not be wise to plant other crops, too, in case the potatoes don't take?' Rose said. She felt a cold hand wrap around her heart as she said the words and a shiver go up her spine.

"'Why?' Albert pointed to the healthy green plants. 'Potatoes grow well in this soil. I've never had them not take.'

"'Yes. You're right. I'm just being foolish.' Rose was leaving the garden when suddenly she pointed to a yellowed, withered leaf.

"'What's that?' she asked.

"Albert bent down and pinched off the leaf, then tossed it away. 'Been a bit dry,' he said, and continued to weed.

"But Rose stared at that lone leaf for a long time, wondering why it filled her with such fear.

"She soon found out, as day by day, more leaves

began to yellow and wither. The potatoes turned black in the fields. The stench of their rotting filled the air and there was no harvest that year . . ." I paused, took a deep breath and let the horror Great-grandmother Rose must have felt fill my voice. "Or the next, or the next. Rose and Albert and their six children grew thin from hunger. All of Ireland was starving and the English landlords would not share their grain, but shipped it back to England." I spat out the words now, as bitter as the Irish people must have been.

"Albert tried to work on the public roads for a bit of money to buy food, but he was too weak. He could barely stand, let alone lift a shovel of dirt. Then one night, returning home after a full day's work on the road, he fell and could not get up." I dropped my voice to a whisper. "He died in the road.

"As dark came on, Rose searched for him and found her husband dead on the very road he had helped build. She buried him in the churchyard where so many of their friends and family now rested. She buried him next to their first baby boy. In the days that followed, two of the children also died and were put in the ground next to their father. Winter came on and Rose tore up Albert's pants to make warmer clothes for the children, but she kept one patch for herself as a remembrance of her husband. My grandma got that patch and sewed it into her quilt."

I pointed again to the blue scrap.

Aunt Ida dabbed at her eyes with a handkerchief.

"You near broke my heart. How do you know all these stories?"

"Mam's mother—my grandma—used to tell us the stories in the Irish Quilt all the time. Mary, Ernest and Fred got sick of hearing the same old stories again and again, but I never did. I guess I heard them so much they're inside me forever now."

"Well, you tell them better than any story that's been written down," Aunt Ida said.

Written down. It hit me so hard, I felt dizzy. I couldn't recall ever seeing Mam's mother write or read anything. She always told us everything.

Aunt Ida grabbed my hand and squeezed it tight. "Rose," she said vehemently. "Never let anyone tell you you're not smart, and if they do, don't believe them. You are special."

I had to smile at tiny Aunt Ida looking so fierce.

Mam appeared in the doorway. "James is looking for you, Ida. He says it's time to head home."

"This girl is special," Aunt Ida repeated to Mam. She stood up, then leaned down and kissed my cheek. "Remember what I said," she whispered. Then she was gone.

"Are you feeling better?" Mam laid a hand on my forehead.

"Yes. Mam, did Grandma know how to read?"

Mam straightened the bed covers. "I never thought about it before, but no, I don't think she could. She always had me read any letters that came. She'd tell me what to fetch from the store and such. Anything that needed writing, I did it for her. Maybe no one taught her how. I imagine Great-grandmother Rose was too busy trying to feed them to have time to teach them their letters."

Or maybe she had, but Grandma couldn't learn to read—*like me.*

"Everyone's leaving the party now, so you get some sleep and you'll be right as rain come morning. Don't forget your prayers."

She turned to leave.

"Mam . . ."

She turned back.

"Could you sing that bedtime blessing you used to when I was little?"

Mam rolled her eyes but leaned over the bed and sang softly. *"Four corners to her bed. Four angels at her head. Mark, Matthew, Luke and John. God bless the bed that she lies on."*

After Mam left, I stared for a long time at the cross on the wall above the dresser. *Am I special, God?* I wanted so badly to believe I was, but Patrick's jeering face shoved its way into my mind. I hoped he stuffed himself so full of sweets he got sick tonight. I fell asleep during my prayers, knowing full well I'd have to confess yet another mean thought.

• • •

"Father McManus came and graced our house last night," Mam said to Da. "You could at least grace his in return."

Every Sunday morning Mam would take Da to task about going to Mass. As usual, we were rushing around getting ready for church. Services started the same time every Sunday, but it was Mam's endless frustration that she couldn't get Ernest to straighten his tie, or Bertie's hair to lie flat—so we were always late. We'd pile out the door, throwing coats over our arms, and run through the streets to St. Joseph's Church. Mam brought up the rear, threatening to give us all a good hiding. Every Sunday it was the same.

Da rubbed a hand through his thinning hair, exasperated with Mam.

"Why don't you like church, Da?" Winnie asked.

"It's not the church I don't like," Da told her. "It's the collar."

"Is it too tight on your neck?" I asked. Mam starched Da's and the boys' collars every week.

"Not my collar. The collar at the front of the church."

"Michael!" Mam was outraged that Da would speak about the priest in such a fashion.

"Oh, very well, I'll come this morning." Da gave in. He knew Mam would be in a vexed mood all day if he didn't. Pots would be banged on the stove. The dinner blessing would be overly long and pious. And we'd have to take messages from Mam to Da all day, as she would refuse to talk directly to him.

"You can't just go to church when you please," Mam said. She wrestled Bertie into his coat. "God doesn't like you coming to church just when you please."

Da's eyebrows lowered into a straight line. Now he was getting into a rage. "Did you get that from God directly, Alice?"

Surprised, I looked at Mam. Did she actually speak directly to God? More important, did He talk back to her? Maybe you had to be a grown-up to have God answer your prayers.

Mam sucked in her breath in horror. "Why you aren't struck down by lightning where you stand . . ."

I know what God looks like. I have since my first communion when I swear I saw Him high in the church arches smiling down at me. I pictured Him now, perched on a cloud, lightning bolt in His hand, looking down from Heaven in search of a sinner. His face is as lined as Grandpa's, though I imagine He has all His own teeth. He has a flowing white beard and kind blue eyes. When He smiles, the day is sunny, but when He is mad, thunder shakes our house. But while I did know what God looked like, I did not know what He sounded like as He'd never spoken directly to me. Would His voice boom like a thunderclap, or be soft like rain misting my face? Perhaps Mam knew.

"Do you want me to come or not?" Da threatened.

"Suit yourself."

What would suit Da would be to meander down the street to visit with Grandpa and have a smoke, but Granny would be yelling Grandpa into his Sunday clothes so there would be no peace there, either. Mam and Da didn't often go at each other, but when they did, it was almost always about religion. I don't think God would be pleased that He was the main cause of cross words in my house.

With a dark look at Mam, Da went into the bedroom.

"There's a fresh collar in your drawer," Mam called after him.

We arrived at church a few minutes late, hastily dipped our fingers in Holy water, bent our knee and crossed ourselves, then slipped into a back pew.

"Last in, first out," Fred whispered to Da.

Mam glared at him but placed herself firmly next to Mary. Mary looked about desperate-like, but being in the middle of the pew there was no escape from Mam. The whispering started soon afterward. Mam automatically stood, kneeled, sat, crossed herself and spoke the responses, all the while scolding Mary for having an Anglican beau.

The Anglicans lived on the south side of Halifax, or so it seemed to us Roman Catholics. Their houses were larger and the wives had maids to do their housework.

Many of the men, like *Horse*, had motor cars to drive. Catholics lived in the north end of the city. Our houses were small, some strung together like beads in a necklace, with no yards in between. Our streets were cinders and dirt, and rang with horse hooves and rattled with wagons. The women kept their own houses and the men left at dawn to work at the docks and rail yards and factories. They worked for the men of south Halifax. Still, as Da often told us, it was the people who dirtied their hands that actually made the city work.

I pushed those thoughts aside and sat quietly, letting Father McManus's words float over me. I drew the scent of incense into my lungs and momentarily felt at peace. Then the well-worn anxiety set in. I still had not written my composition, nor had I done my reading, and I had to face Sister Frances tomorrow.

I bent forward and stole a glance at Mary, but her sour face told me I wouldn't get any help from her. Aunt Ida and Uncle James sat in the pew in front of us, and I toyed with the idea of asking her for help, but she thought I was special and I didn't want her to find out how dumb I really was. Mam would be busy with Sunday dinner, and Winnie and Ernest weren't patient enough. Martha sat to the side of us. She'd help me, but her mother wouldn't let her out on Sundays.

Why couldn't I just write the story myself? I knew what I wanted to say. I wanted to write about the terrible hunger in Ireland that had forced my great-grandmother Rose to come to Canada. I wanted to write about the dreadful ocean voyage she endured. The words made sense in my mind, but I couldn't get them to make sense on paper.

Chapter 7

I closely followed the back of the girl in front of me through the heavy front doors into the school. We'd been at St. Joseph's Church for a special service. I had tried to take the opportunity to ask God for help with my story, but the older girls had giggled in the back pews. Next thing I knew, I found myself asking that He let them be friends with me and I forgot about my story.

As I passed the white marble statue of the Virgin Mary sitting at the foot of the stairs beside the piano, I glanced at her serene stone face. She'd probably never felt the fear and embarrassment of standing in front of the class, stumbling through a reader. I sent up a fervent prayer to the Virgin to get me through this day in one piece. I didn't think God would mind if I asked for her help, too, as I imagined He was pretty busy, what with the war and all. The thought crossed my mind that I certainly asked for a lot for myself. I debated for a moment if this was something I should confess, then decided not. Surely God wouldn't want to be bothered with every little might-be-a-sin I committed.

"Step lively, girls." Sister Frances prodded my back.

I noticed she didn't single anyone else out, but I

wanted to stay on her good side today, so I hurried up the stairs, only to catch my foot in the hem of my dress. I went down flat on my face, arms outstretched, legs flailing.

"Can you not even walk properly?" Sister Frances stood over me, hands on her hips.

"Sorry, Sister," I murmured. I staggered to my feet, hauling my skirt out from under me, but I yanked too hard and sent it and my pinafore flying over my head.

"Pull your skirt down! You're indecent!"

"Sorry, Sister." I wrestled the skirt back down, my face red as Mam's pickled beets. My heart sank. I knew what this meant. I had displeased God with my selfishness. This did not bode well for the rest of the day.

Giggles filled the hall. I glanced back in time to see Martha speak behind her hand to the girl beside her. They both laughed, and a pang of hurt shot through me. I vowed right then and there that if Martha couldn't be friends with me in school, we wouldn't be friends outside of school, either.

I made it into the classroom and into my seat without any further catastrophes.

"Feet on the floor. Hands in front."

Dread squeezed my heart. I had spent Sunday struggling with the words in my reading assignment, an ordeal that had taken the entire afternoon, but they were committed to memory. Then I had tried to write my composition. I told myself I could do it if I really tried and wasn't lazy like Sister Frances thought me. I wrote one word, erased it, wrote another and erased it, too. By the end of Sunday evening I had one-and-a-half sentences and a big hole in the paper from erasing so much.

Sister Frances walked up and down the aisles, checking the insides of our ears. As she exclaimed over one girl's dirty ears, "You could grow potatoes in them," I sent up one final prayer. *Please, God, make it so Sister Frances doesn't ask to hear my composition. I'll never ask for anything more for myself again. I promise.*

He must have heard me, because Sister Frances didn't once call on me. Her pointer slapped down on other girls' desks, but not mine. Then, magically, it was morning break. I floated out of the school, knowing I was especially blessed today. It didn't matter what I did, God would take care of me. I eyed the girls from my supposed-to-be-in class. Martha smiled back at me. Another sign. Taking a deep breath, I walked over to them. Martha's smile faded and her eyes widened in dismay. She shook her head at me, but I ignored her. She couldn't know I was especially blessed today. That was between God and me.

"Hello," I said. The girls exchanged glances and sly smiles. My brain froze. I couldn't think of another thing to say. I suddenly realized that I had made a terrible mistake. I had overestimated my blessedness.

After a long moment of silence, Catherine spoke. "I see you're wearing your skirt down for recess."

A burst of laughter. Martha studied her feet. I smiled, pretending to join in the joke. "That was just a silly accident," I said. *Please, God, let my feet leave before this gets worse.* A second realization swept over me, more dire than the first. I'd just broken my promise to not ask for anything else for myself. God made my feet take root as punishment.

After a moment, Catherine said, "We're talking about some grown-up things. You wouldn't understand."

"I—I'm as old as you are," I protested.

"Well, yes and no. You might be in years, but you are two grades below us in brains," Catherine explained sweetly. She turned her back on me. "I had a letter from my father," she told the girls. "He can't come home because he's very important to the war. He's a general, you know. He's in France and is sending me some fine silk material for Christmas to make a dress for me."

I looked to Martha for help, but her shoes continued to hold her mesmerized. I didn't know what to do.

"No one from your family is overseas, are they, Rose?" Catherine suddenly asked.

I shook my head.

"I thought not. Some fight, others don't. I expect my father will arrive home with a chest full of medals," she said.

I wanted to tell her about Da and Fred and my uncles working hard on the docks, all for the war effort, but couldn't find the words. Finally, God took pity on me and let my feet loose. As I walked away, I put my hand to my cheek and it came away wet. The sky was clear, so the wet wasn't rain. *How could You let me cry in front of the girls, God?*

"You can play with us, Rose." Winnie had seen the girls—and the tears.

I held my head high. I wouldn't cry in front of Winnie's baby friends. "Never mind, Winnie. I'm still not feeling good from my cold. The wind is making my eyes water."

By the time we went back into school, the blessed feeling had completely worn off. Sunk deep in misery, I didn't hear Sister Frances until her pointer whacked across my desk and made me jump.

"Take the cotton out of your ears, Rose. Stand and read the story you wrote."

I picked up my reader and flipped through the pages with sweaty hands. At least I had it memorized.

"Not from your reader. Listen!" Her hand tweaked my ear and I yclped with pain. "The story you *wrote.*"

I fumbled with my scribbler as she moved a few desks away. My one-and-a-half sentences looked lonely in the middle of the mostly empty page. I held the book up high so Sister Frances couldn't see them. Part of my brain registered the classroom door opening and a rustle of cloth. Who had left the room? Or had come in?

My hands shook. Suddenly I knew what to do. I'd tell the story. It was right inside me.

"Ireland was starving. It was 1847 in the middle of the famine." I moved my eyes from side to side to pretend I was reading. "My—My great-grandmother Rose—Rose," I repeated, stumbling over the words. "She could not earn money for food for her four children and my great-grandpa Albert was dead." Slowly I picked up the rhythm of my story and the words flowed more easily.

"One day the bailiff came to the cottage. 'The English landlord says you will have to leave,' he said.

"'Where will I go?' asked Rose.

"'The poorhouse,' said the bailiff. He didn't care where Rose went, as long as she left.

"But Rose knew if you went into the poorhouse, you never came out again—alive. She went to the village priest, who gave her money to go to Canada. Rose made a small bundle of her belongings and gathered up her four children. With thousands of other evicted tenants, they walked many days to the seaside, Rose carrying the youngest child. My grandma, who was four years old, walked all the way." I finished in a rush and sat down, relief weakening my legs. I had done it. I had *read* my story.

"Yes, well. Very good," Sister Frances said grudgingly.

I smiled at her.

"Please turn in your scribbler so I can check your spelling." Sister Frances held out her hand.

The smile slid from my face. *Turn in my scribbler?*

"Now, Rose."

I couldn't move from my seat.

A huge black cloud, Sister Frances sailed down the aisle toward me. Every head turned to watch as she passed, though no one made a sound. An angry Sister Frances was not to be crossed. She stopped in front of my desk. I tried to slip my notebook underneath my reader, but she snatched it away. The paper crackled as she flipped to the page where I'd written my one-and-a-half sentences. Her nostrils flared.

"Stand up," she yelled.

I scrambled to my feet.

"This is your story?" She jabbed the page with a stubby finger.

"Yes, Sister," I whispered. "I had trouble writing it down. It was all in my head, though. It really was, so that's almost like writing it."

"Trouble writing it? You have used no punctuation, there are no spaces between your words—if you can call these scribbles that look like a chicken crossed your page *words*. No one could make sense of this—this . . ." She threw the book down on my desk and thrust her face into mine. "Do you know what you are? Do you know what you are?" Spittle flew from her mouth to my cheek, but I dared not wipe it off.

Terrified, I shook my head.

"You are a liar. A lazy liar and a wicked girl. You are

a wicked girl," Sister Frances repeated. "And do you know where wicked girls go?"

"Yes, Sister," I mumbled. "They go down there." I pointed to my feet.

"Yes. They go directly to Hell."

To Hell? I thought she had meant the principal's office on the floor beneath us.

I heard a soft gasp from the back of the classroom. I wanted to turn and see who was there, but Sister Frances hit the side of my head a stinging blow.

"Go to the principal and take your scribbler. You will give her a full explanation."

The other students were completely silent, shocked to see right before them a girl headed to Hell. Ear ringing from the slap, I ran out of the room. I ventured one quick sideways glance to see Sister Therese at the back of the classroom, face distraught. It was she who had come in earlier.

As I closed the door, pent-up tears streamed down my face. I had disgraced myself. I had disgraced Mam and Da.

The principal's office door was closed, so I stood beside it in the hall. School let out for the morning and still the door remained closed. The girls filed by, tossing curious glances my way, but no one spoke to me. Miserable and scared, I kept my eyes on the floor. I wished I could pray, but I found I couldn't. Didn't want to, in fact. Praying had got me into this mess in the first place. If I hadn't asked for so many things for myself, God would never have needed to punish me. I had no one but myself to blame. But still . . . I felt let down.

"I'm disappointed in you, God."

"I beg your pardon?" Sister Therese had come up behind me.

"Nothing, Sister," I mumbled.

"Oh, Rose." She sighed. "You are in a spot of trouble. Can I see your notebook?"

I handed it to her and hung my head in shame. I knew what she was seeing: black ink blots, half-formed words, holes in pages where I'd erased so many times the paper was worn away.

"Every time I use a pen, I break the nib or the ink spatters. I tried to use a pencil, but I erased too much," I said. "I can't write the words, though I know what I want to say . . ." My voice trailed off.

Sister Therese closed the scribbler. "I suspect the problem may be that you see things differently than we do, Rose," she said. "I've had other students like that."

The door to the principal's office opened. Sister Maria Cecilia came out and directed a raised eyebrow my way. "Why are you here?"

My heart pounded.

"Sister Frances sent me," I said.

"May I see you a moment before you speak with Rose?" Sister Therese asked.

The principal nodded, and Sister Therese carried my

notebook into the office and closed the door behind her. A few minutes later she came out, notebook gone. "The principal will see you now," she said. She laid a reassuring hand on my shoulder, then went down the hall.

I went into the principal's office, sure she must hear the loud thumps of my heart. They deafened me. Sister Maria Cecilia sat behind the desk, my notebook open in front of her. She studied it for several moments, then leaned back and folded her hands out of sight inside the sleeves of her habit.

"Well?"

I stuttered and fell all over my words as I tried to explain. When I finished, she turned page after page of my unsightly work. Finally, she closed the notebook.

"Lying is a terrible habit to get into and, like most habits, difficult to break," she said sternly.

I nodded. Father McManus would give me a stack of Hail Marys and Our Fathers for this one.

"I will send a note home to your mother and father. Sister Frances says you are lazy and inattentive, though Sister Therese does not share that opinion. She says you try hard but find it difficult to learn. She's offered to give you extra help if you wish." Sister Maria Cecilia opened a desk drawer and took out a piece of paper. "Either way, I'm very much afraid you will be kept back at the end of the year if your work does not show marked improvement between now and then."

"I can't be kept back again," I protested. "I'll be in my little sister's class if I'm held back."

"This type of thing won't do, Rose." She gestured toward my notebook. "You can't write or spell or do proper arithmetic. We can't possibly allow you to go on to the next grade when you're obviously not ready. You can step into the hall and think about that while I write this letter to your parents."

I did as she asked and waited outside the door. What would the letter to Mam and Da say? I suddenly held my head up. That was it. I was never coming back to school. Never. And I wouldn't take this letter home to Mam. In fact, I wouldn't go back home at all. I'd—I'd go into service like Aunt Helen had suggested. My thoughts skidded off in every direction and my chest heaved as I tried to make plans.

Winnie pounced on me as soon as I left the school.

"Did you get a whipping, Rose?" she asked. Her eyes were like saucers. "Everyone said you'd get a whipping. They said you'd done something awful. A mortal sin, Catherine said."

"I didn't get a whipping, and how on earth would Catherine know what a mortal sin is? She's not even Catholic," I yelled at Winnie.

"What happened, then?"

"Winnie, leave me alone. Go home. You're not to tell Mam or Da about any of this."

"But where are you going?"

The boys were starting to arrive for their afternoon classes. I was afraid I'd see Ernest—or worse, Patrick. I had to leave, fast.

"I just want to be alone for a little bit," I told Winnie impatiently. "Tell Mam I . . . had an errand. I'll be home soon."

Winnie took off down the hill at a run, wild with excitement. I knew she'd tell everyone she met that I had got a whipping, even though I hadn't. That was just Winnie. I wouldn't be able to show my face for a year. The older girls would never talk to me now, but it didn't matter as I was never coming back. I walked rapidly in the opposite direction from our house. Tears started up again, though I told myself to stop. I didn't cry pretty like Mary. I looked a frightful mess with red-rimmed eyes and a runny nose. But I couldn't help myself. Right there in the middle of the road I sobbed. I didn't know where to go. There was no place to escape *me*.

Chapter 8

You can't stand in the middle of the street crying, I scolded myself. What if Great-grandmother Rose had stood in front of her cottage in Ireland and wept instead of getting on the ship for Canada? I knew what I had to do. I just had to find the gumption to do it. I closed my eyes a moment and tried to picture the way Mary and I had gone on the streetcar to the south side of Halifax. I could see in my mind the stores and houses we passed, the turns we made. It would take me longer to walk, but I felt confident I could find my way. Once there, I would hire myself out as a maid at one of the big houses. It would mean leaving Mam and Da, but I pushed that thought right out of my head.

I started on my way before my brain could tell me I was scared. Wind whipped up from the harbour, biting cold, but three days into December had seen little snow. I pulled my coat close and walked rapidly to keep warm. A small thrill ran through me. An adventure. I walked past shops and peered in the windows. I enjoyed the feel of the hard sidewalk beneath my boots rather than dirt. A sidewalk made me hold my back straighter, and, I thought, lent me an air of importance.

Then, all at once, my stomach growled and my legs ached and the skies opened to pour an icy rain on me. Thoughts of Mam setting out bread and preserves haunted me. She would pour hot tea from the brown everyday pot. Suddenly, I felt as if I'd been away for years.

A good part of the afternoon had passed when I stopped in front of a large, white-framed house. I looked up and down the deserted street. My neighbourhood bustled with life; women called to each other from their doorways as they shook out mats and mops, delivery wagons crowded the streets and children darted everywhere. The quiet here made me vaguely uneasy.

As I had walked from north to south, the houses had become larger and farther apart. It would be a pretty street in the summer when the trees were in full leaf, but right now it looked bare and unfriendly. I stepped up to the fence surrounding the house and peered over it. A porch stretched across the entire front. Mam would like that. She'd often told Da how nice it would be to have a porch out front rather than a step to sit on in the warm weather. Da had said he'd make her one when he had a spare moment. Mam had replied she wouldn't hold her breath in that case. It was like I'd left them already.

Wet through, I shivered violently as I shifted from foot to foot, wondering how to approach the house. Did I go to the front door or the back? I had heard somewhere that maids didn't go in front doors in big houses.

In fact, we seldom used our front door at home, even though we had a small house. I craned my neck to see into the side yard. There was a door there. Would that do? I lost my gumption at that point and moved down the street. I stopped in front of each large house I came to, but I couldn't force my feet to go up to any of them. What if the woman there asked me a question and I didn't know the proper answer? What if they asked me to read something—like a shopping list? No one would hire a girl who couldn't read a shopping list.

I arrived at the last house on the street, and stood in the shelter of the trunk of a large tree. I felt desperate now because I'd wasted so much time, so I took a step into the yard. A blur of snarling fur flew around the corner of the house. I turned and ran as fast as I could. I darted a quick glance over my shoulder to see if I'd outrun the dog, then crashed into someone, fell and rolled across the lawn. I propped myself up on hands and knees to see a young girl being helped to her feet by an older one. Paper, pencils and a school bag littered the lawn, flung from the force of our collision. I scrambled on all fours to gather up the now soaked scribblers, and shoved them back in the bag. I stood and held the book-bag out to the little girl.

"Sorry," I muttered.

The older one snatched it out of my hand and glared at me. "You should be more careful. What are you

doing here on our property?" she asked. She looked to
be my age.

"I . . . I . . ."

"You don't come from around here," she said.
"She's not from around here," she repeated to her
younger sister. "That's a poor girl's coat."

Surprised, I glanced down at my jacket, new to me
this year, even if it had been Mary's at one time. All in
one piece and with no patches—I couldn't see anything
poor about it. The two girls were dressed in matching
navy coats with red hats, though the younger girl's tilted
over one ear from her fall. They weren't hand-me-
down coats. The older girl had gloves, the younger one,
mittens. I envied her those mittens as my hands were
numb from cold.

"Does your mother need a maid?" I asked. I cringed,
fearing her answer. I hoped her mother did, but I hoped
more that she didn't.

"A maid?" The older girl laughed. "You don't look
like a maid to me. You're covered in mud and you are
far too skinny."

She pushed past me and went up the sidewalk toward
the house. The younger girl stared at me curiously.

"Did I hurt you?" I asked.

"No." She smiled a bit. "Are you cold?"

I nodded.

"Do you want to come in for tea?"

The older girl ran back, grabbed her sister's hand and gave it a vicious shake. "You don't ask maids in for tea!" She turned to me. "You better go now or I'll tell my mother."

I knew her type. Another Catherine. "Bossy," I whispered.

The younger girl grinned while the older one glowered at me. I quickly backed away and hurried down the street. I didn't want to be a maid anymore.

The December afternoon darkened rapidly. Blackout regulations because of the war meant no street lights and house windows draped in heavy curtains. I stumbled, unable to see clearly. I had walked too far. My legs would never carry me back to our warm kitchen. I'd never see Mam or Da again.

Head lowered against the rain, I put one foot in front of the other. A motor car passed, its wheels throwing up a sheet of water. I jumped aside, then realized it didn't matter. I couldn't get any wetter. Horses' hooves rang on the road beside me. *Please, God. Let me get home safely. If You do, I'll never ask for anything again.*

"Rose?"

My heart stopped. God had answered me directly.

"Rose Dunlea? Is that you?" For some reason, God sounded like Duncan.

My befuddled brain soon told me it was Duncan. He pulled up on the horses' reins and stopped the milk wagon.

"What are you doing here?" I asked.

"Finishing my milk deliveries, but more importantly, what are you doing here? Does your mother know where you are?"

A sudden picture came to me of Mam wild with worry. Ashamed I hadn't thought of that before, I shook my head. To my dismay, I began to cry.

Duncan jumped down from the wagon and lifted me up onto the seat. He whipped off his coat and wrapped it around me. "Let's get you home before you get pneumonia."

We rode in silence for a few minutes, Duncan shooting worried glances at me. "Well, your lips aren't quite so blue now," he said.

I did feel warmer wrapped in Duncan's coat, though my teeth chattered non-stop.

"What are you doing so far from home, Rose?" he asked.

My voice shook and my nose dripped as the story poured out of me: the composition about Great-grandmother Rose, how I couldn't read, Sister Frances, the letter for Mam and Da, becoming a maid, the girls in the navy coats. As I talked I watched his eyebrows lower until they formed an angry straight line above his eyes. He was mad at me. He thought I was dumb.

"D–U–M–B," I spelled out loud. Strangely, I knew I had got it right.

"Who's dumb?" Duncan asked.

"I am." Tears flowed. I'd had no idea there was so much water in me. I must have saved up an entire year's worth just for today.

Duncan fished in his pocket and handed me his handkerchief. I mopped my eyes, balled it up and pushed it into my coat pocket.

"I didn't know you delivered milk this far away," I ventured after a while.

"It's not far when you're riding." He smiled at me, and I felt a tiny bit better.

"We deliver all over Halifax. Our dairy's well known," he said, a hint of pride in his voice.

"Do you deliver to Horse's house?"

"Who?"

"I mean Horace's house. He lives here."

Duncan's face clouded over. "I might. Which one is his?"

"I don't know," I said. "Mary would know. She's been to it."

Duncan's eyebrows raised in surprise. "Horace had her over to his house? For tea? Supper?"

"No," I replied. "No one else was home. He was just showing it to her. Mary's ambition is to live in one of these big houses."

"Is it, then." His voice sounded bleak.

"She says people can't stay in the north end all their lives. It's limiting, she says," I prattled on. It occurred to me that Mary might not like her ambitions being discussed with Duncan, but now that my tongue was loosened, I couldn't keep it still.

"The north end is my home—and hers," Duncan said. "I'm not saying I wouldn't want to see more of the world. I would. But I will always come back home. It's where I'm most comfortable."

"Me, too," I told him.

Houses crowded closer together now and the yards were shrinking.

"Nearly home," Duncan said.

My stomach knotted. Mam would be furious.

"Rose!" A shout came from the side of the street. Then Fred ran alongside the horse. Duncan slowed, and Frederick jumped up beside me on the seat.

"Where have you been? Where did you find her, Duncan?"

"In the south end," Duncan replied. He started the horse again and turned down our street.

"In the south end! I'm the woolgatherer who's supposed to get lost. Not you, Rose," Fred said.

"I wasn't lost," I protested. And that was true. I hadn't been lost. I knew where I was the whole time.

"Mam is fit to be tied," Fred continued. "She's got everyone out looking for you. Even Aunt Ida and Uncle James."

"Is she terribly mad, Fred?" I asked.

"I think she's ready to give you a good hiding." He grinned, reached an arm around my shoulders and gave me a hug. I leaned in to him.

We pulled up in front of the house. Ernest was in the yard and immediately ran into the house when he saw us. Soon, Mam flew out, Bertie holding tight to her apron strings. Granny, Aunt Ida and Winnie hurried after her.

"Look what Duncan found." Fred jumped off the seat and helped me down.

Mam pulled me into a tight embrace. "You had us worried half to death. I should give you such a hiding."

I looked up in time to catch Fred's wink.

"She's done in, Mrs. Dunlea," Duncan said. "She walked all the way to the south side."

"Why on earth would you go there?" Mam began. "Never mind. Let's get you warmed up and then you can tell us what happened."

Mary ran up the street, out of breath. Even through my worry and tiredness, I couldn't help but admire the colour in her cheeks. So did Duncan, I could see.

"Hello, Mary," he said.

"Duncan brought me home," I told her.

"From where?" Mary asked.

"I went to the south side. I probably passed Horace's house," I said.

Mary flushed a brighter red at the mention of Horace. Duncan's eyebrows lowered again.

Mam steered me toward the house. "Fred, you and Ernest find Da and the others and tell them Rose is home safe."

"Wait," I told her.

I unwrapped Duncan's coat from around me and gave it to Mary. She stared at it, then handed it up to Duncan. He dropped it beside him on the seat. With horror, I realized he'd been in his short sleeves all that time in the cold rain.

"Thank you for the coat and ride," I called over my shoulder.

"Rose," Duncan shouted back. "You're not D–U–M–B."

Mam swept me into the kitchen before I could answer Duncan, but it didn't matter. His words gave me the first warmth I had felt all day. Mary got out the tin bathtub, while Aunt Ida built up the fire and set kettles on the stove to heat.

"That girl will get the influenza or the rheumatic fever for sure now," Granny announced solemnly. She plopped herself down at the kitchen table and put a hand to her chest. "Perhaps a cup of tea? All this worry is bad for the nerves. I'll get the heart trouble."

"You should be home, away from the excitement," Aunt Ida said soothingly. "And won't Helen be wondering what's happened?"

"You're right. Poor Helen. I should put her mind to rest." Granny's eyes brightened as she thought of all the news she had to tell. She bustled into her coat, stuck a pin through her hat and headed out the door.

"Thank you, Ida," Mam said. She stripped my wet clothes from me and handed them to Mary, then wrapped me in a large towel and rubbed briskly. "And you just getting over your cold . . . The south side . . . A good hiding—that's what you need."

Winnie helped Aunt Ida fill the tub, and I climbed in, sighing with pleasure as the heat hit my cold skin.

Winnie leaned over the tub. "Did you see some big houses? Were you running away from home? Is it because of Sister Frances?" Her eyes shone with excitement.

"Winnie, you are in my way," Mam scolded.

Aunt Ida pulled Winnie aside. "Leave Rose be just now. You can run up and get her nightgown. The warmest one she has."

A short while later, I sat at the kitchen table with Mam and Aunt Ida, my hands wrapped around a warm mug of tea, heavily sugared—"for the shock," Mam said. Winnie sat on the floor and played with Bertie, though I knew she was bursting to get me alone. Footsteps rang on the porch steps. Da was home. My heart pounded as Da, Fred, Ernest and Uncle James came in. Mam might threaten a hiding, but Da stirred up might give one. Da stopped and looked at me, then turned, took off his coat and hung it up. Mam got up and put the kettle back on the stove.

"Turning right miserable out there," Uncle James said. "Ida, we should be getting home."

Aunt Ida nodded and pulled on her coat. As she passed me, she bent down and kissed my cheek. "Be a brave girl," she whispered. No two ways about it, Aunt Ida was definitely my favourite aunt.

Mam took Da and Fred's dinner from the oven and set it on the table. Da nodded his thanks and Fred tucked right in. Neither said anything to me.

"Ernest, take Bertie upstairs and get him ready for bed," Mam ordered. "Winnie, you go up, too."

Winnie opened her mouth to protest, but one look at Da's face closed it right fast.

The kitchen emptied. I could hardly breathe as I watched Da eat. He finished and pushed back his plate. Mam set his tea down, then sat at the table next to him.

Fred looked from Mam to Da. "Excuse me," he said, and headed to the porch for a smoke.

"I'm glad to see you're home safe," Da said. He took a sip of tea, then banged his cup down on the table. I jumped.

He leaned toward me. "Do you know how worried we were about you? Your Mam nearly out of her mind? Everyone looking for you?"

"I'm so sorry, Da," I said. I wouldn't have believed it possible to squeeze out any more tears, but I was wrong. They flowed down my face.

Da looked twice as upset at making me cry. "Hush

yourself, then. I only wanted you to understand how you worried the whole family. What were you doing in the south side?"

"Looking for a maid's job like Aunt Helen said," I sobbed.

Da looked at Mam, puzzled.

"She was here the other day and said Rose should get a job as a maid rather than go to school," Mam explained to him.

"Helen," Da stated flatly.

"Oh, you know Helen," Mam said soothingly. "She says whatever she thinks. I didn't know Rose overheard." Mam raised her eyebrows at me. I'd hear later about the evils of eavesdropping.

I went to where my coat hung by the stove to dry, and rummaged in the pocket. I pulled out the letter from Sister Maria Cecilia and handed it to Da. He read it, then passed it to Mam, who quickly skimmed it and uttered a small moan of dismay.

"Da, I really tried to write the story. I really did," I told him. "I spent all Sunday after Mass working on it and my reading, but I couldn't get the words to come out properly. Sister Frances says I'm lazy and simple—"

"She says that?" Da interrupted. His fingertips drummed on the table, a sure sign his temper was rising.

"Yes, but I'm not lazy, Da." I had to convince him. "I really do work hard, but I can't get words to make sense when I write them down. I get all the letters mixed up."

I could see by their faces they didn't understand. No one could.

"Da, please don't send me back to school. I hate it there. I have no friends. Everyone thinks I'm slow. Sister Maria Cecilia says I have to be held back again." I began to sob.

Da pulled me onto his lap. "Hush. Hush, my Wild Irish Rose." After a moment, he said, "You're never to do anything this foolish again, do you understand?"

I nodded.

"Get to bed. You've had enough adventure for one day."

Halfway up the stairs, I stopped to listen. As I already had the sin of eavesdropping to confess, I couldn't see how doing it twice would make it worse.

"Blasted nuns," Da said.

"Michael!"

"Alice, they got her all defeated."

There was silence, then Mam spoke. "Maybe it would be best if she stayed home. Next year she'll be fourteen and she can hire out as a laundry maid. Or she might even find work in the textile factory. I imagine Ida could help her get a job—"

Da broke in impatiently. "I want better for her than doing other people's laundry, Alice. Look how well Mary's doing."

"Is she?" Mam's tone was dry. "I don't know that Mary working at that bank is making her any happier than the other girls around here."

Da's mind was still on me. "Rose needs to stay in school until she's sixteen."

"She's so unhappy, Michael."

"She'll do fine. She's just taking a bit longer to learn. It'll come to her all at once, and then you'll see. She'll outshine all the others."

Mam sighed. "I'll go to the school tomorrow morning and speak with Sister Frances and the principal. Maybe something can be worked out. I don't want her held back again. I don't think she could take it."

"See what you can do, then," Da said.

I heard their chairs scrape across the floor and I flew up the stairs and crawled into bed beside Winnie. I closed my eyes and said my prayers, and ended with a final, desperate one. *Please, God, make it so I don't have to go to school.*

Chapter 9

I wiped porridge from Bertie's face, holding him firmly by the chin as he squirmed to get away from the wet flannel. Mam had left me in charge while she went to the school to speak to the principal. I knew once she saw how awful Sister Frances was, she'd get me special permission to leave school. Normally, you had to be past grade seven or fourteen years old, but sometimes younger children got permission to stay home, if needed. I knew that was how God would answer my prayer—with special permission.

The kitchen door banged open and Ernest and Patrick dragged a sled into the room.

"Can I go sledding, too?" Bertie asked Ernest.

"Not today. There's no snow. I'm just fixing it up." He searched in Mam's cleaning closet and surfaced with steel wool. "Grandpa said there would be a good fall by Saturday and he's usually right." Ernest upended his sled and began scraping the runners with the steel wool.

"You're making a mess," I shrieked.

"I'll clean it up after," Ernest said, not the least bit bothered by the rust flakes drifting to the floor.

"Put a cloth underneath it. If Mam sees that dirt she'll be so mad . . ."

"She'll give me a good hiding," Ernest finished cheekily.

I got an old sheet Da had used to cover the sofa when he painted the parlour. "Lift it up, " I ordered.

Ernest picked up his sled and I placed the sheet beneath. Patrick wandered around the kitchen, his ever-present candy bag in one hand.

I poured a kettle of hot water into the dishpan and swished in slivers of soap to wash up the breakfast dishes. I wanted everything perfect for Mam's return. Once she saw what a help I was, she'd want me to stay home. But there was still Da to get around. I shrugged. I had every confidence in God—and Mam.

"So why are you home, dummy? The Sisters finally decided you're too stupid for school?" Patrick asked.

I washed a cup and ignored him, remembering how that had really bothered him at the park.

"She's so stupid, they won't even let her into the school." Patrick spoke to Ernest but his eyes slid my way. I washed a bowl.

Silence certainly left Patrick at a loss. He rapped Bertie on the head—hard—and held out the paper bag. "Want a candy?"

Bertie winced and rubbed his head, but reached out eagerly. Patrick pulled his arm back. He put the bag to his lips and blew it up, then burst it with a *bang*. Bertie's face collapsed into tears.

"That was just downright mean, Patrick." I rapidly dried my hands. "You should be on your best behaviour. Christmas is just twenty days away and you know Santa Claus is watching to see if you're good."

"Who cares?" Patrick laughed.

"Well, then you should care that God is watching," I told him.

He grinned, reached into his pocket and popped another candy in his mouth.

I got Mam's cookie jar from the pantry and handed a cookie to Bertie. "Never mind, now. He keeps eating all that candy, he's just going to be a fat pig."

"He already is," Ernest said.

"Take that back," Patrick shouted.

"Fat pig," Bertie repeated happily.

Ernest took a cloth and wiped a runner. "You'll be so heavy your sled won't carry you. You'll be left at the top while all we boys fly down the hill."

"Shut up. All of you, just shut up!" Patrick's face turned purple with rage.

"That's quite enough of that language." Aunt Ida came into the kitchen, bringing with her a blast of damp, cold air. "Your Mam asked me to look in," she said.

"A convoy's forming up," Patrick muttered to Ernest. "Do you want to go see?"

"Sounds fine," Ernest said. He and Patrick were ship mad. They drew ships and built models of ships and painted ships. Ernest had been kept in after school for having more pictures of vessels in his scribbler than spelling words.

He ran upstairs and grabbed the binoculars Mam and Da had given him for his last birthday. Back in the kitchen he pulled on his coat. "Let's go."

"Wait," Aunt Ida called. "Put away your sled and the cloth."

"I'll do it when I get back." Ernest smiled broadly, half out the door.

"Do it now," she ordered.

I could have hugged her for not letting Ernest's smile get him his own way. Grumbling, Ernest hauled his sled out to the backyard, while surprisingly, Patrick folded the sheet neatly and set it on a chair.

"You know, Rose," Aunt Ida said. "I still have my coat and hat on. Maybe we should take Bertie for a little walk and join the boys and take a look at that convoy ourselves."

If Aunt Ida had told me she had a notion to go for a little walk on the moon, I would have gone right then with her.

"Do you have to go with us?" Patrick groaned.

"It'll be nice for us all to go together," Aunt Ida replied.

We walked to a small, grassy rise that gave us a view

of both Bedford Basin and the Narrows, the channel that connects Bedford Basin to Halifax Harbour. The convoys, sometimes as many as forty ships, would form up in Bedford Basin. White clouds scudded across a hard blue sky, casting dark shadow ships over the water. Wind pulled at the waves, tipping them with white froth.

Ernest peered through his binoculars. "That's the H.M.S. *Highflyer*," he announced excitedly. He pointed at a cruiser. "It's British. It sunk a German ship."

"Let me see now," Patrick whined. He made a grab for Ernest's binoculars, but Ernest twisted away.

"Ernest, perhaps everyone could have a turn," Aunt Ida said.

Reluctantly, Ernest handed his binoculars to Patrick.

"Merchant ships over there being loaded." Patrick nodded toward the docks, not wanting to be left out. He lowered the binoculars. "You know," he said to Aunt Ida, "there's an anti-submarine net across the harbour. They close it every night so no one can get out or in, especially enemy submarines."

"You don't say . . ." Aunt Ida shook her head in wonder, as if she'd never heard of that net—though I imagine, like everyone else in Halifax, she knew all about it. "I'm sure Bertie would like to see the boats now."

All plumped up with importance, Patrick immediately turned over the binoculars to Bertie. Aunt Ida smiled her thanks at him, and Patrick blushed bright red. For a wonder, he even helped Bertie hold the binoculars.

After a few minutes, Aunt Ida handed them to me. It took a moment to focus them, then I found a ship. "There's a big one called the *I–M–O*." I spelled it slowly. "There's something painted on the side. *B* . . ."

"Here, let me see. You'll take all day." Patrick snatched the binoculars from my hands.

Spitting mad, I tried to grab them back, but he held them out of reach.

"I'll have a turn now." Aunt Ida held out her hand. With a grimace at me, Patrick passed over the binoculars.

Aunt Ida focussed them on the ships. "It says, *BELGIAN RELIEF*. It's taking on coal, so she'll be leaving soon," she said. "It's a first-aid ship. It'll have blankets and medicine for those poor war refugees in Europe." She handed the binoculars back to Ernest. "Thank you, dear," she said. "Rose, we'll take Bertie back now and get some lunch started so Ernest won't be late for school. Watch a few more minutes, then come directly home, Ernest."

As we walked back to the house, I plunged my hands into my pockets to warm their icy tips. Feeling a lump in one, I pulled it out and saw I still had Duncan's handkerchief. I would wash and iron it before I gave it back. I pushed it down in my pocket again, and began to think.

Duncan had been around all my life. He was nearly family. I would like to have a piece of him in my Irish Chain quilt. I wondered if he would miss the handkerchief if I kept it and didn't say anything. I debated whether or not that would be considered stealing. I could see myself pointing to his patch in my quilt and telling my children the story of how Duncan had rescued me from the south side of Halifax. I would keep Duncan's handkerchief, I decided. Now, if I had found Sister Frances's handkerchief, I would have given it right back to her. Same with Patrick. I've asked God why He made some people so vexing, but He hasn't answered me yet.

"Patrick isn't very nice sometimes, is he," I commented.

"I don't imagine it's easy being Patrick," Aunt Ida said.

I stared at her in surprise. Not easy to be Patrick? With a candy bag in his hand all day long and no chores to be done?

"It must be tiresome being an only child and having all that expectation and attention placed on you. And being overweight. I imagine the children at school tease him. He probably doesn't have many friends."

I hadn't thought about it before, but I had heard the boys teasing Patrick. And other than Ernest, I'd not seen Patrick with any friends. In fact, Ernest was Patrick's only friend. He wasn't any more popular than

I was. I kicked at a stone in the road. Well, I certainly was not going to feel sorry for him. He brought everything on himself by being so mean and miserly. Patrick was a bully through and through. No wonder no one liked him.

We passed the Protestant orphanage and Bertie stopped to watch some boys throw a ball in the yard.

"Can I go play with them?" Bertie asked.

"No, dear," Aunt Ida told him. "That's the orphanage. Those children live there, but you don't, so you can't go in."

"I'm glad I'm not an orphan," I announced.

"You're very fortunate to have a large family," Aunt Ida replied. "It would take some doing for you to become an orphan. Some of these children, though, aren't real orphans. Some have fathers in the war overseas and when the men return they'll be together again as a family."

That made me feel a bit better to think the children weren't all alone in the world.

I grabbed Bertie's hand and squeezed it tight inside my own. "I'll play ball with you when we get home," I promised.

We walked in silence and my mind returned to my own problem. It was like a sore that I wanted to pick and pick at. Would Mam get special permission for me to leave school? And if she did, what would I do?

"Did you like working in the factory?" I asked Aunt Ida.

"It's not the easiest work, but it pays well. For a woman, that is."

"Are you glad you don't work there anymore since you married Uncle James?"

"Sometimes I am, because as I said factory work is hard, but I had a good time with the other girls. I miss that. It gets lonely at home on my own."

"But you can always visit us," I pointed out.

"That's true."

"Would I like factory work?" I persisted.

"I think you could do better than factory work, Rose," Aunt Ida said.

"Aunt Helen says I should go into service."

"Wouldn't you like to have a typewriting job like Mary?"

I shook my head. "I would have to finish school and then go to a secretary's school like Mary did." Just what I needed, more school.

"You should finish school," Aunt Ida said. "It gives you more opportunity. I often thought I might like to be a nurse, but my father died and my mother was ill. I left school to support her, though she didn't last too long. You finish school, Rose. Then you can take your choice of what to work at."

I grimaced. "That's what Da says."

"He wants the very best for you. All of you."

I sighed. It seemed all the adults in my life wanted me to finish school. Why couldn't any of them understand? I could never get a job as a typist. It'd take me all day to write one letter and even then I'd have to go back and fix the spelling a hundred times. When I first started school I had thought I'd like to be a teacher. I had let that dream go in fairly short order, though a stubborn part of me foolishly held on to a bit of it. Right there on the spot, I suddenly wanted to tell Aunt Ida that I'd like to be a teacher, but I stopped myself. It seemed too silly.

"But why go on in school if I'm just going to get married and stay home?" I asked.

"Not everyone gets married," Aunt Ida said. "And now with the war on and so many men away, the women are doing their jobs. A woman should be able to support herself and not rely entirely on a man. What about your great-grandmother? She must have had to work to support her children."

I nodded. "She ran a boarding house when she got to Halifax. At first she helped out, but eventually she owned it herself."

"Every woman should be able to do some kind of work. I think you could be anything you put your mind to, Rose. Don't sell yourself short."

Mam had arrived home before us. She slapped pots noisily on the stove and muttered away to herself.

"That infernal woman . . . the nerve . . . pigheaded and stubborn—"

She caught sight of us. "Do you know what that—that nun said to me?" she spluttered. Her eyes darted angrily from me to Aunt Ida. "She said . . ." Mam stopped, then turned back to the stove. "Rose, run upstairs a minute and . . ." Mam floundered. "And give your hair a good brush. It's all wild from the wind."

I stared at her open-mouthed. I'd had my scarf on all morning and my hair was flat against my head. "But Mam—"

"As I say, Rose," Mam said.

I slowly climbed the stairs, then stopped. I began a moral fight with myself. I'd promised God I wouldn't eavesdrop ever again, but these were special circumstances. Surely He would understand that. I needed to know if Mam had got special permission. I sat down on the step.

"That Sister Frances," Mam said. "She is dreadful. She called Rose . . ." Mam's voice dropped to a whisper, so I strained forward to hear. ". . . retarded."

My heart plummeted all the way down to my toes. I'd known all along. Catherine and Patrick had called me that, and I had tried to put it down to them being mean. But to hear Mam say the word made it real. I slowly climbed the rest of the stairs to the bedroom. The Irish Chain quilt still lay on my bed, and I wrapped myself and my misery inside it.

As I sat there, I realized I still didn't know if Mam had got special permission for me to stay home. Maybe school didn't even want me back. I hadn't listened long enough.

I clattered down the stairs and burst into the kitchen.

"Rose," Mam exclaimed, "you're dragging that quilt on the floor. You'll ruin it."

"Sorry, Mam. I felt a bit of a chill." And that was true. Sister Frances's words had left me cold. I folded the quilt carefully and put it on the settee.

I was exasperated to see Winnie, Bertie and Ernest eating lunch at the table with Mam and Aunt Ida. I couldn't talk to Mam with them there.

"That's a beautiful quilt, Alice," Aunt Ida said. "How precious it must be to you, knowing it was made by your mother. And all those small pieces of material. Such a lot of work."

Finally, Ernest grabbed his bag of school books. "I'm off, then," he said. He kissed Mam on the cheek. "See you later, twerp," he told Bertie. "Keep an eye out for snow while I'm gone."

"I will," Bertie promised happily. He settled down by the window, intent on catching sight of the first flake.

Winnie wandered over to the settee, sat and spread out the quilt. "Tell us this story, Rose." She pointed to a light blue square of cotton.

I was about to tell Winnie to go play with her friends, when I realized that after a story she'd leave on her own.

On the other hand, if Winnie knew I wanted to speak to Mam, curiosity would make her as hard to budge as a rock.

"Stories are for bedtime," Bertie said.

I sat beside Winnie and pulled Bertie on my lap. "You *are* going to bed. For a nap. Now listen, because this patch is from our own grandma's dress that she had when she was as little as you. She wore it on the ship when they came to Canada."

Bertie laid his head against my chest as I started the story. "With hundreds of other desperate Irish, Rose and her remaining four children crowded onto a ship bound for Canada. Huddled below deck, the air was foul and there was little room to move. Many people were sick—some with inflammation of the lungs, some with fevers, some close to death and all, starving. It was a ship of skeletons, the passengers being nothing but skin and bone. Rose had bought food to keep her children fed on the long voyage, but it soon disappeared, so Rose did without so her children wouldn't starve. Terrible storms pitched the ship. The wind screamed above deck and great seas washed into the hold, where Rose and her children were locked in for days on end."

As I told the story, Mam's warm kitchen darkened, grew cold and damp, and rocked as if tossed on ocean waves. "The baby could not keep food down. She burned with fever. Twenty days into the voyage, she died and was given to the ocean. Now Rose only had three children left—the youngest was our grandma, who was four. To ease their fears and her own, Rose sang to them night after night. After seven weeks, Rose and her three children saw land." I paused to let the fact that the sea voyage was over sink into my listeners' heads. "It was Canada. They sailed up the St. Lawrence to a tiny island, Grosse Île, in Quebec. At first relieved to be on firm land, Rose was soon dismayed to learn they would be quarantined on the island, as many of the people on board ship were ill. Rose's first home in Canada was a small corner of a crowded stone shed."

My words fell into the silent kitchen. I drew in the fragrant smell of bread, and the room stopped its heaving and brightened.

Aunt Ida drew a shaky breath. "It's uncanny the way you tell a story, Rose. I almost feel like I'm there. It's a gift, Alice, that's what it is, and if those nuns at that school can't see that . . ." Aunt Ida shook her head.

"Winnie, would you take Bertie up and settle him for a nap," Mam said. "Then you can go play."

Aunt Ida got to her feet and pulled on her coat. "I better be seeing to my own house," she said.

Then there was just Mam and me in the kitchen.

"Did you get special permission?" I blurted out.

Mam looked bewildered. "What special permission?"

"To let me stay home. To not have to go to school

anymore. If you tell them you need me at home, I can get special permission to leave school."

"Oh, Rose," Mam said. "You know your Da won't let you leave school. You shouldn't have pinned your hopes on that." She stood and gathered the dishes. "I'll help you with your spelling. We'll show Sister Frances what a good pupil you are."

I stared at Mam in disbelief. *But I'd asked God to let me stay home.*

"Mam," I said, "does God really answer people's prayers?"

A terrific *thump* from overhead took Mam to the bottom of the stairs.

"What is all that noise up there? Winnie, I told you to put Bertie to bed."

"I am, Mam, but he keeps getting out. I'm trying to hold him in."

"I'll go help Winnie." I got up wearily from the table.

"Rose." Mam's voice stopped me. "Yes, He does answer people's prayers, but not always in the way you expect."

Chapter 10

I woke early Thursday morning, even before Mary got up to catch the morning car. A crack in the curtains showed the beginnings of a rose-pink dawn, though a silver night star still shone bright. The scent of sausage, eggs and potatoes frying made my stomach growl. I hadn't eaten much supper the night before. I could hear the low rumble of Da's and Fred's voices as they ate breakfast. I untangled Winnie's legs from mine, but stayed in bed despite my hunger. I didn't want to see Da. In fact, I hadn't spoken to him all last evening. I knew he was hurt, but I was afraid if I opened my mouth all my anger would pour out.

I heard the outside door open, a flurry of goodbyes, then quiet. I crawled over Winnie's sleeping body and widened the crack in the curtains. Da and Fred strode down the street to the rail yard, lunch pails swinging at their sides. Da suddenly shot a look over his shoulder at the house, like people do when feeling watched, but I quickly drew the two halves of the curtain together and sank back onto the bed.

"What are you doing up so early?" Mary stretched and yawned.

"I have to go to school," I told her.

"You go to school every day, but you're not usually up this early."

I shrugged and left the room. I didn't want to talk to Mary today—Mary who only had time for Horace and his Roadster. In the kitchen, Mam sat at the table with a cup of tea in front of her. Kettles of water steamed gently on the stove.

"I thought you were Mary," Mam said. She stood up, took her cup to the stove and refilled it, then took down a second cup and poured tea for me. "It's such a fine day out. Good to do the washing."

I flopped into a chair across from her. "I could stay and help."

"You have school, my girl," Mam said firmly. "I know it seems like forever you have to go, but it's really just a short time. You'll be all grown up before you know it, with your own house to keep."

I grimaced to show her what I thought of that idea, then slurped my tea just for good measure.

Mam laughed. "You'll see. Things change quickly in life. Sometimes in a minute it seems. Now, would you run and tell Mary to hurry herself, or she'll be late for work. Then you can pull Winnie out of bed for school."

I passed Bertie on the stairs, his eyes and legs heavy with sleep as he bumped down step by step on his backside. "Tell me a story, Rose?" he asked hopefully.

"Stories are for before bed, not when you get up," I told him.

As I climbed the last few steps, I wondered if Great-grandma Rose had had days when even her bones felt tired. Probably. On the sailing ship to Canada, she woke each morning to hungry children, the stink of hundreds of unwashed passengers and endless ocean. Grandma had told me how awful it was: awful enough for her to remember, even though she was only little.

As I went into our bedroom, I wondered if Great-grandmother Rose had wished she had a dove the way Noah in his ark had. She could have sent it out to find Canada, so she could get off the boat. My brain told me her troubles were worse than mine, but I couldn't help but feel adrift on my own flood of misery. I wished I had a dove.

And what about Noah? I flung myself on my bed and watched Mary rush about with hairbrush and pins. Noah must have been sick of those animals after forty days of living with them. Did he despair each time his dove came back, its feathers wet? But then, one day the dove had a green leaf in its beak. *Hope.* I shook my head despondently. Maybe in Bible stories that's how it was, but not for Great-grandma Rose—and not for me. I still had Sister Frances to face this morning. I glanced at the small cross over the bed I shared with Winnie, then averted my face. I saw no point in saying my morning prayers. I shook Winnie to wake her.

In the kitchen, Ernest filled Mam's washing machine with the now hot water. "Hurry up, Winnie," I urged. Usually it was me who dawdled, but this morning Winnie couldn't find her school slate.

Suddenly the kitchen door burst open with such a *bang* that we all jumped. The stove hissed as Ernest spilled water from a kettle.

Patrick rushed in, then bent in half, his breathing coming fast. He gripped the side of the door to hold himself upright. He must have run all the way to our house—and Patrick never ran.

"What's the matter?" Mam asked, alarmed. "Is your mother unwell? Granny?"

"Ernest," he gasped, "two ships collided in the harbour. Smoke and flames everywhere."

"Wow! Can I go see, Mam?" Ernest asked. He grabbed his coat and slapped his cap on his head, and was out the door before Mam could say yes or no. Through the half-opened door I heard shouts and yells from the street.

"Can I go, too, Mam?" Winnie shoved her arms hurriedly into her coat.

Mam shook her head. "You'll make yourself late for school."

"Aw, Mam." Winnie deflated like a balloon. "Ernest gets to do everything," she whined.

"School is more important. There'll be other fires," Mam told her.

"I'll be right back, Winnie." I ran upstairs with an old shirt of Fred's that Mam had pulled from the wash and pronounced only fit for the rag bag. I tugged open the lid of the chest and stuffed it into my bag of patches for my quilt. I would cut a piece from it later.

I lingered at the window, drawn by the tower of black smoke rising straight into the sky with no wind to carry it away. With effort, I dragged my eyes away and went downstairs.

I gave Mam a quick peck on the cheek. "Come along, Winnie," I called. I didn't want to start the day off in Sister Frances's bad books.

The street was full of people running toward the harbour. A siren wailed as the fire department's new motorized truck screamed by.

"Did you see that?" Winnie yelled. She jumped up and down excitedly. "It went so fast."

Women stood on their steps, drying wet hands on aprons. Men on the way home from the night shift gathered in small clusters to point at the smoke and discuss the collision. Legs pumping, boys raced down the street. The din was incredible. As I neared the corner, I swore I could hear Granny's chickens clucking, all caught up in the uproar. Granny and Aunt Helen stood in a group of women in the middle of the road, their own beaks going a mile a minute. Grandpa leaned against the milk wagon speaking to Duncan. Winnie ran over to them, and I reluctantly followed.

"Well, little Winnie and Rose," Grandpa said. "Big doings at the harbour. So many ships they can't keep out of each other's path it seems."

I could tell by the way Grandpa slurred his *s*'s that he had not stopped to put in his teeth.

"Grandpa. Can I go down to see the fire?" Winnie asked.

"Winnie," I scolded, "Mam already said no."

Winnie scowled at me.

"I'd like to go see, myself," Duncan said. "But there are people waiting for their milk delivery."

He slapped the reins against the horse's flank. "Have a good day at school, girls."

There was no such thing as a good day at school, I wanted to tell him, but by the time I thought to say it, he was gone.

"Winnie, we have to go." But my feet couldn't move as I watched a ball of yellow fire climb up inside the black smoke. I shivered and wrapped my arms about myself.

"Holy cow! Did you see that? Can't we just go look for a minute? Everyone else is. I bet Fred and Da are watching," Winnie begged. "Look at all those people on the roof over there. I bet they can see everything."

I shook my head and grabbed her hand. A sense of urgency moved my feet quickly toward St. Joseph's School, and it wasn't all fear of Sister Frances. I was suffering an attack of the nerves, as Granny would say. We arrived to find the schoolyard deserted.

"See, now we're late. Just because you had to stop and look," I hissed. I gave Winnie's arm a sharp poke.

Winnie stuck out her tongue at me and ran into the school. I followed, hurrying past the statue of the Virgin Mary and the piano to the stairs. Catherine and Martha climbed in front of me. I wasn't surprised to see Catherine—she wasn't Catholic, so the Sisters excused her from morning prayers—but Martha was late like me. They turned at the sound of my steps.

"Why, Rose. I really didn't think you'd be coming back," Catherine said.

"I don't know what would make you think that," I said airily.

Martha ducked her head and looked ill at ease. Well, I thought, she should. How could she be my friend one day and not the next? A fair-weather friend, that's what she was.

"Well, you have so much trouble with your school-work and all, because you're slow, and your mother was here yesterday to see the principal," Catherine went on.

She made me so mad, I swear my blood boiled. I pushed past them both, head held high. "I have every intention of getting an education. I'm planning to work in a bank like my sister Mary."

Catherine might have a war hero father in France, but she didn't have a sister who worked in a bank.

We had reached the top of the stairs. My classroom

was off to the right, Catherine's and Martha's to the left; we shared a cloakroom at the back of the hall. Catherine gave me a small shove as she went to hang up her coat.

"Girls." Sister Frances stuck her head around the classroom door. Her eyes narrowed angrily. "You're late and you're interrupting morning prayers. Get your coats off immediately and get to your classrooms."

I scurried to the cloakroom. Catherine and Martha had hung up their coats and were walking rapidly to their class, Martha ahead of Catherine. My fingers fumbled with buttons as I struggled to remove my jacket. Sister Frances had the effect of making me all thumbs. I suddenly looked up, alert. Too quiet, the air too still, then, no breath in my body. A brilliant flash. A tremendous *boom*. Weightless, I flew backward into the cloakroom. Windowpanes sucked inward and shattered. Sharp silver darts fell on my head and arms. I instinctively raised my hands to protect my head. Walls collapsed and plaster rained down as the building exploded. Then, utter silence and blackness. I'd been struck deaf and blind. Someone screamed. *Me?* No— Catherine, I thought. On and on she shrieked, then others joined. I wished I couldn't hear.

I tried to open my eyes but the lids stuck together. Panicked, I clawed at them. My fingers came away sticky wet, but at least I could partially see again. Through swirling dust, I could make out the shadowy form of Catherine laying outside her classroom door. A large portion of the floor between us was gone. She screamed again.

"Stop it," I croaked, then said more loudly, "Be quiet!" I crawled toward her, keeping to the perimeter of the cloakroom and hall. I didn't want to be sucked down into that black hole. I stretched out a hand and wrapped my fingers around Catherine's wrist. "Stop it." I shook her arm. It was important she stop screaming, because I still wasn't sure it wasn't me making that terrible noise.

"Where's Martha?" I asked.

"I don't know." Catherine gasped. "What is it? What happened?"

A loud *crack* brought our heads up to see a large section of the floor in the classroom behind Catherine give way. Girls and desks plunged to the floor below. Dust thickened again and closed my throat. I coughed so violently I thought my lungs would burst. On hands and knees, I felt my way to the stairs. Catherine gripped my skirt, and I dragged her behind me. Still crawling, I made my way down the sides of the stairs, avoiding the empty spaces where steps had disappeared. Somehow I made it to the bottom. Through the gloom and dust, the white marble statue of the Virgin swayed back and forth in a frightening ghost dance—*Winnie*. I had to get to Winnie in the downstairs classroom. I shook Catherine off me and stumbled through the hall over

crushed desks and plaster and bodies. Suddenly a beefy
hand gripped my wrist so hard I yelped with pain. Nails
dug into my flesh.

"Get on your knees. Pray! Pray, you wicked girl. It's
the end of the world."

Sister Frances had hold of me and would not let go. I
kicked and struggled. A snap from the ceiling distracted
her momentarily. As she loosened her grip on my arm,
my fingers found the beads and cross about her neck. I
twisted them and broke the chain. Sister Frances
released me with a cry of rage.

I scrambled away from her on all fours. Above me,
the roof dipped and white plaster drifted down. I feared
it might cave in on me. I'd be no use to Winnie if I got
trapped inside the school. I saw that the lid of the piano
tilted toward a window. I could slide down it and out
into the yard.

"Help me," Catherine screamed.

I debated leaving her, then turned back. I pulled her
up and shoved her to the piano. "Get up on it," I
ordered.

Surprisingly, she did as I said and slid on her back
down the lid of the piano and out the window. Another
girl took her place, and I helped her, too, to slide out the
window. I started to follow, when a voice in the gloom
stopped me.

"Is someone there?"

It was Sister Therese.

"Yes, it's Rose," I answered.

"Rose, I can't see, but I've brought some of the little girls from downstairs. Can you help them out?" Sister Therese asked calmly.

A chain of girls was attached to her habit, each holding the next one's hand. One by one I slid them down the piano top and out the window, then helped Sister Therese onto my makeshift slide. I followed her into a nightmare.

Nuns and girls lay on red-stained ground, some moving, others still. Many wandered about aimlessly. It was eerily quiet, the only sound an occasional moan or a *crack* as the collapsed school shifted. As soon as she saw me, Catherine latched onto my skirt again. Nothing could remove her, so I pulled her along with me as I searched.

"Winnie! Winnie!" I yelled, my voice overly loud in the silence.

As I rounded the corner of the school, I saw her seated beneath a tree, arms wrapped around her body. I ran up to her.

"Winnie, are you hurt?"

She rocked to and fro and raised her head, but her eyes remained unfocussed. I tried to examine her, but she wouldn't unwrap her arms from her knees. As best I could see, she had some cuts and bruises but no serious injury. I pulled her to her feet.

"What happened?" Martha came up beside us, eyes

wide and frightened in a face covered in dust. I barely recognized her.

"I don't know," I told her. "How did you get out?"

"I was in the doorway," she replied. "I think it protected me. The whole room went down. Our classroom. I followed you and Catherine down the stairs. Then you slid me along the piano lid," she said. "Right behind Catherine."

In my fear and confusion, I hadn't realized Martha was behind us, or that I had helped her out the window.

We stared at our ravaged school. Walls were half collapsed, the cupola on top tilted crazily to one side. The front door swayed drunkenly on its hinges. A few men reached the school and ran into the building. They staggered back a few minutes later with girls in their arms, leaving red-ribbon trails on the ground behind them.

My mind was ice-clear. I knew what I needed to do. I needed to find Mam and Da. They would help me wake and end this nightmare. For that was all this was—a nightmare.

"Let's go home, Winnie," I said.

Winnie said nothing, but her body shuddered violently. I took off my sweater and buttoned her into it, though I had to pry her arms from her sides to do so. I knew I should feel cold as I only had my blouse sleeves, but I didn't feel anything. Not cold, not pain, even though blood ran down my arm and dripped from my fingers.

"You're bleeding," Catherine said. "On your arm and head."

Somehow she still held onto my skirt. I tried to pull it from her hand, but she held tight and I didn't have the energy to fight her.

"You're bleeding," she repeated.

I examined the flap of skin hanging above my elbow. White bone showed beneath, but I felt as if I were looking at someone else's arm, not my own.

I noticed then that Catherine's white-blonde hair was streaked red. "You're bleeding, too," I said.

She put a hand up to her head and began to wail. "I want to go home. I want my grandmother."

"Go home then," I told her brutally. Maybe now she'd let go of my skirt.

She looked around bewildered. "But where is my house?"

Every house, store and building was flattened as far as I could see. The sugar refinery, the tallest building on the waterfront, had vanished. Panic rose in my throat. I turned to find the church, my place of safety, but even it, God's house, was destroyed. We huddled closer together as we stared at the frightening landscape before us.

Catherine whimpered. "I can't find my house."

"Everyone together now." A nun from the convent next to the school herded children before her into the yard. "Your parents will be here soon to get you."

I looked out at the destroyed city. What if Mam and Da couldn't get here? What if they couldn't find their way? I thought of Sister Frances's death grip on my arm. I knew how grown-ups were. Once they got hold of me, they'd never let me go and find Mam or Da. I remembered the way to our house. I could see it in my mind. I could find it even with the streets and houses gone.

"Come on, Winnie," I said. Catherine and Martha crowded behind us. "Why don't you go with the nuns," I told them.

"Please, let us come with you," Martha said. "Please, Rose. I'm scared."

"Fine, but keep up," I agreed reluctantly. I felt sorry for Martha-with-no-gumption, though it would take some doing to feel the same for Catherine.

I closed my eyes and pictured the school, the streets, Catherine's house, our own, until I had it so clear in my mind that it was a shock all over again to open them and see the devastation.

"A white picket fence," I said to Catherine.

"What?"

"Your grandmother's house had a white picket fence around it. Ours did, too—"

"Girls." A nun headed toward us. I quickly moved away, Winnie, Catherine and Martha at my heels.

Chapter 11

My eyes saw terrible sights: a woman hanging lifeless over a windowsill; a man crushed beneath the collapsed wall of a house; a girl leading her little brother, his face a bloody pulp; a dray horse dead under the wagon it had recently pulled. My eyes saw all this horror, but my brain did not register it as I calmly picked my way over the rubble. I did, though, have the presence of mind to pull Winnie close to me and bury her face in my coat. I couldn't be sure whether she shared my nightmare or not. She shivered uncontrollably now, her skin a pale shade of blue that worried me desperately. I would take Catherine home first, I decided, as she was closest, and I would be rid of her. Then I'd find Mam and Da so they could help Winnie. Martha, I'd worry about later.

We stumbled along, me with Winnie in my arms, Catherine gripping my skirt and Martha behind. The silence was unnerving, the only sound a bell tolling in a church spire. One Christmas I had been given a set of wooden Pick-Up Sticks as a gift. You threw them down willy-nilly and then tried to carefully pick each up without moving another. I felt like I'd walked right into the middle of a giant's game of Pick-Up Sticks: trees uprooted, telephone and electric poles snapped off, all tossed together haphazardly. Few buildings stood, and the ones that remained had windows that stared at us emptily and rooms that were sheared off with a bed or an enamel bathtub exposed. Wires spit sparks and I made a wide circle around them, though I didn't slow my speed. I followed a map in my mind. Black smoke billowed from where the sugar refinery had once stood. I used it as my landmark in this unfamiliar world. I squinted up at the sky to see a yellow ball through a thick grey haze—the moon, I thought at first, then realized it was the sun. A million hours seemed to have passed since I got up that morning, though it had been only a few.

A man ran up to us, chest and arms bare. His hair and face were drenched in a black oil, through which his eyes shone brilliant blue, and wild. Martha and Catherine immediately stepped behind me. I tightened my grip on Winnie.

"Where am I?" he panted. His eyes roved frenetically. "What street is this?"

I stared at his chest, pumping in and out like a bellows.

"The Germans. They bombed us from their airships. The war's come to us." He cringed and looked into the sky. "Look! There they are. The airships."

I followed his pointing finger but didn't see anything.

"Where am I?" he repeated. He reached for me, but I stepped back, terrified.

"Run," I yelled. I grabbed Winnie's hand and pulled her past the man. Frantic minutes later, I stopped to get my bearings. Our mindless flight had disoriented me. I closed my eyes for a moment to bring up the picture of our neighbourhood.

"Germans. That man said the Germans did this," Catherine spat at Martha. "Look what you've done to us!"

"It wasn't the Germans," Martha said. "At least, it wasn't *us*. We're Canadians. My family are Canadians."

"You're all spies. If my father was here, he'd get rid of you all," Catherine told her.

"Shut up," I yelled. I didn't care how rude I sounded, I needed to concentrate. It suddenly came to me where we were.

"Your grandmother's house is right here," I said.

"But there's no house." Catherine's voice trembled. "And where's my grandmother?"

I picked up a few pieces of broken, white fence, then threw them down again. This was definitely the right spot. Beams, plaster, shattered glass, a chair with a broken leg and shingles were all that remained. A small curl of white smoke rose from the wreckage that had been Catherine's home. A moment later, a lick of yellow flame shot up and took hold, no doubt fed by the coal in the overturned kitchen stove. What flitted into my mind was that Catherine's grandmother might be beneath that pile, but I didn't pay that thought much heed. I couldn't.

"Grandmother! Grandmother!" Catherine circled the yard. She gave a cry and plunged her hand into an opening in the rubble. "Look what I found." She held up a doll, china head miraculously intact. She cradled it in her arms, crooning over it, and seemed to forget her grandmother.

I stared at the growing flames, felt their heat on my face, and my feet wanted to fly home.

"Maybe your grandmother is away," I told Catherine. "I think you should go back to the school and wait for her. Maybe she'll come looking for you there."

"No," Catherine said stubbornly. "I'm going with you."

I sighed, but I'd already wasted enough time. I had to get home. "You can come with me," I told Catherine, "but you can't hold my skirt. I can't walk properly." At least I'd solved one problem.

People streamed by us, some silent, others sobbing quietly, all dazed and shocked. Women in house clothes, no coats or boots, carried injured children in their arms. I tried not to look, but my eyes were drawn to the broken bodies. Men in nightshirts, recently abed from the late shift at the docks, tore at their destroyed homes with bare hands, shouting their wives' and children's names. We passed a man stripped of every article of clothing, except for his cap. Fear rose in my throat at this strange new world. *A nightmare*, I reminded myself. When I found Mam, she would wake me.

"Patrick," Winnie whispered, the first words she'd spoken.

How she recognized him, I don't know. He, too, was covered in the black, oily slick. I noticed then that he only had one shoe, his other foot bare.

"Where's your stocking and boot, Patrick?"

It was the only thing I could think to say.

He looked down at his foot, surprised. "I don't know," he said.

"What's all over you?" Catherine demanded.

"It rained black," Patrick replied.

Suddenly, I remembered Patrick barrelling into our kitchen with news of the ships' collision. I remembered red and yellow flames and dense smoke in the early morning sky. Patrick and Ernest had gone to look at the fire, and only Patrick stood in front of me now.

"Where's Ernest?" I asked him.

"What?"

"Ernest—where's Ernest?"

"He's run home to get his binoculars so he can see the ships better. He should be back any minute now," Patrick said.

"What happened at the harbour?" I asked.

He shook his head but didn't reply. I wanted to cuff his ears in hopes it might make his brain work.

Finally, he gathered himself together. "We went to see the ships. The fire. We started down the street, but Ernest said he needed his binoculars and went back home and then—" Patrick stopped and ran a pink tongue around his black lips. "I flew through the air. My ears hurt badly. Something hit my head, hard." He rubbed the side of his head and his hand came away red mixed with black. "Next thing, I found myself up here, though I don't know how I got here because I was down close to the docks." His lips quivered as he relived his fear. "There was no one around. I thought everyone was dead except me." Tears trickled over his oil-slick cheeks. "But Ernest should be here soon."

"Flee!" The voice yelled so close to me that I jumped.

A soldier roughly shoved my back, and I staggered into Winnie.

"Run!" he cried. "The magazine in Wellington Barracks might go up at any moment. Get to high, open ground!"

People screamed and swarmed frantically by us on all sides. Children yelled for their parents. Patrick was thrown to the ground and trampled underfoot. I crouched over Winnie to protect her. *A nightmare*, I assured myself. *I will wake up.* In horror, I watched a woman crawl by, one leg dragged behind, useless.

All of a sudden Martha gave a cry and threw herself into the arms of a man. "Papa, Papa."

Mr. Schultz scooped her up and continued to run up the steep hill with her in his arms. I stood to get their attention, but Martha didn't look back once.

"Well, I, for one, am glad that German is gone," Catherine announced.

"Shut up. Just shut up." I lashed out at Catherine, though I wasn't really mad at her. I was mad at Martha. Once again, she had deserted me. Mr. Schultz was the only familiar adult I'd seen today, and Martha hadn't even bothered to tell him about us.

Patrick scrambled over the ground on all fours. "My cap," he said. "Where's my cap?"

"Never mind," I said. "We have to go."

"But my mother told me I should wear my hat at all times. She'll be mad if I lose it."

I hauled him to his feet. We stumbled along with the hysterical crowd, away from home. Suddenly, I grabbed Patrick's arm and pulled him and Winnie to squat behind a tumbled-down wall. Catherine followed. Did I know whose home this was?

"I'm going back to find Mam and Da," I said. "If we don't go now, they'll keep us away forever. No one would notice us, not in all this confusion."

"But what if there's another explosion?" Patrick protested.

"We'll just have to chance it. Don't you want to go home?" I asked him.

Patrick looked doubtful but didn't object further.

"The soldier said we were to go to open ground," Catherine reminded me primly.

"So, go," I urged her. "Maybe your grandmother is there."

Catherine hugged her doll. "I want to stay with you," she muttered.

From beneath a shattered bureau, I pulled out a man's boot. "Would this fit you, Patrick?" I asked. He needed something to protect him. There was so much glass on the ground, his foot would soon be cut to shreds.

He slipped the boot on. "It's a bit big, but it'll do grand," he said.

"We'll have to stay hidden as much as possible and avoid the soldiers," I said.

"How?" Patrick asked. "Everything's flattened. There's nothing to hide behind."

"Just do your best, but follow me. I know where I'm going."

"How do you know—" Patrick began.

"You can follow me and find your house, or go your own way and wander around," I said angrily. It was my bad dream, after all. I could do what I wanted. "I don't care, but I remember the way home." I glared at him and Catherine.

Neither made any move to head out on their own.

I pulled on Winnie's hand, but she wouldn't get up. "Come on, Winnie." I tugged harder. "We'll be home soon." She merely whimpered. Her eyes rolled back in her head.

"We'll have to carry her," I said to Patrick. "And wrap your coat around her. She's shivering."

"I'll get cold," he whined.

"If you want to come with me, you'll give Winnie your coat."

Reluctantly, Patrick stripped off his jacket and wrapped it around Winnie.

"Your arm's bleeding," Patrick said.

"I know," I replied impatiently. Blood from the cut made my hand slippery, but I still didn't feel any pain.

Patrick and I locked our hands together and awkwardly carried Winnie between us. We stumbled over the littered ground. It was hard walking forward with my body bent sideways and I was soon out of breath. Sweat ran down Patrick's face. He wasn't cold anymore, I thought. Or perhaps it was from the searing heat of the numerous fires that raged on each side of us. I tried to speed up my feet and almost went down.

"What are you doing? You nearly dropped Winnie," Patrick yelled.

"The fires," I gasped. "The stoves have overturned in the houses. We have to hurry. Everything will be on fire soon."

Patrick glanced around and increased his speed. He whispered beneath his breath.

"What?" I asked him.

He didn't reply, but continued to whisper. I caught the words.

"Hail Mary, full of grace," he repeated over and over.

I tried hard, but no prayers would come to my lips.

"Not much farther," I gasped. And it wasn't. I knew where I was. Patrick's house was one way; ours, the other. Selfishly, I didn't tell him. I needed his help with Winnie. Another block and I saw the remains of a second white picket fence, blackened now and broken, only the gate intact, flat on the ground. Behind sat what remained of our house—a heap of wood and plaster. Patrick and I stared open-mouthed. I had seen other houses destroyed, but somehow had thought ours would be standing. If you *owned* your house, wouldn't it still stand? I gulped back a sob. *A nightmare, not real,* I told myself, but I struggled to believe.

I set Winnie down on the flattened front gate, then ran to the pile of wood. Smoke and fire poured from the kitchen area. "Mam!" I screamed. "Mam!"

"Rose." A thin moan sounded above the crackle of flames.

"Ernest?" I called.

"Rose."

The voice came from beneath my feet. I began to throw aside boards, and wrestled a twisted bed frame—

one I recognized as my own—away from the pile. I came to a thick beam and tugged on it, but it wouldn't move.

"Patrick. Help me," I yelled.

He hung back. "It's on fire." His eyes were wide with terror.

"I can't lift this and Ernest is underneath."

Patrick didn't move.

"Help me!" I screamed at him. "Ernest is your friend."

Slowly, he climbed over the shattered house. Together we strained to lift the beam. Flames licked around my boots as the fire took firm hold.

"It's no good," Patrick gasped. "It's too heavy."

"We have to get him out. Try again."

Suddenly a hand pushed me aside and a rope snaked around the beam. "Back up! Back, you old nag!"

The rope stretched from the beam to the back of Duncan's wagon. "Rose," he said, "grab the reins and pull her forward."

I ran to the horse's head. Its eyes rolled wildly. Digging in my heels, I leaned all my weight on the horse's head—and it took a step forward.

"Again," Duncan yelled.

"Move!" I screamed. The horse took a second step, then a third.

"That's it! No further or the floor will collapse."

I watched as he stretched full-length and reached into

a hole. A moment later, he hauled Ernest up by the back of his shirt.

I ran over to him. "Ernest. Where's Mam and Bertie?"

"I can't see!" Ernest screamed. "I can't see."

"Get him away from here before this all falls in," Duncan ordered. He leaned back over the hole and called down. There was no answer.

Patrick dragged Ernest to lay next to Winnie on the gate.

"I can't see. My face hurts so much." Ernest's hands clawed at his eyes.

Duncan took a rag from the wagon and carefully wiped dirt from Ernest's face. "He's got glass in his eyes. That's why he can't see," Duncan said softly. He took off his shirt and wrapped it around Ernest's head, covering his eyes. "He needs a doctor immediately."

"Ernest, do you know where Mam is? And Bertie?"

"She went out back to see if she could hang the wash. She didn't want to get ash from the fire on it," Ernest said. His chest heaved for air.

I noticed that he held his binoculars in one hand.

"Bertie was in the kitchen beside the stove."

"We have to find them." I got to my feet, but Duncan held me back.

"It's no use, Rose. No one could survive those flames," he said gently.

I jerked away from him. Mam had been outside,

Ernest said, not in the house. I ran to the backyard. Mam lay on the ground by the kitchen garden. One arm was flung outward, fingers open, beckoning me. I knelt down beside her.

"Mam." I took her hand. It was cold. I'd have to warm her. A cup of tea, perhaps. Mam always said a cup of tea was just the thing.

"Mam. Wake up. I'm having a bad dream, Mam." Why did she lie so still?

"Rose." Duncan's hand came down on my shoulder. He knelt and held Mam's wrist for a moment, then let it drop. "She's gone, Rose."

"No, Duncan," I insisted. "This is all a bad dream. Mam will wake up and make it go away. You'll see."

I shook Mam's arm.

Duncan swung me around to face him and placed both his hands on my shoulders, giving me a little shake.

"It's not a bad dream, Rose. It's real." Tears filled his eyes. "It's horrible, but it's real. It's real."

Of course it was real. Even before he'd told me, I'd known it was real, but hadn't wanted to believe it. Now that the words had been spoken, I could no longer pretend it was a bad dream. I kicked his shin, then pummeled him with my fists.

"You shouldn't have told me," I screamed at him. Suddenly, my body went limp and I slumped to the ground. "My arm hurts, Mam," I sobbed.

Chapter 12

Duncan gently pulled me to my feet, away from Mam. Numb, I followed him back to the street where Winnie and Ernest lay on the gate. Patrick stood motionless, face frightened, as he stared at the destruction all around. Only Catherine seemed oblivious as she hummed and rocked her doll.

"What about Bertie?" I asked Duncan.

"Ernest said he was near the stove last time he saw him. If so"—he gestured helplessly at the burning debris—"he couldn't be alive in that, Rose."

I knew what Duncan said made sense, but a part of me remained stubborn. "We should check," I insisted.

"Rose . . ." Duncan began. He ran a hand through his hair, making it stand on end. Da did that, too, when pushed too far. "It'd be foolhardy to waste time trying to find him. Winnie and Ernest are hurt bad. They need a doctor right away—"

"What about my mama and dad?" Patrick interrupted.

"The entire street is on fire," Duncan said. "The whole north end!" He took a deep breath, then continued more patiently. "They'll be at the hospital. I'm sure you'll find them there. Same with your granny and grandpa."

I could tell by the way he wouldn't meet our eyes that he didn't believe his own words. Patrick wasn't fooled, either, but he nodded and didn't protest. Seeing him give in so easy took all the fight out of me. I sank down beside Winnie. My arm hurt terribly now. Duncan took my arm and inspected it.

"This is a bad gash. You need a doctor, too."

Suddenly, Patrick grabbed the blanket from around Catherine's doll.

"Hey! That's mine," Catherine shouted.

"Rose needs this more than your dumb doll," Patrick said. He wrapped the blanket around my elbow and tied it tightly. "That should help a bit until we get to the doctor. I cut my arm once and Dad put a cloth around it like this to stop the bleeding."

I'd never seen Patrick help anyone before, but I was glad he'd bandaged my arm. The sight of the flap of skin and the white bone beneath had begun to make my head spin.

Duncan looked up and down what remained of the street. "There's others here hurt. So many—" His voice cracked, overwhelmed with the enormity of it all. "Well, I got the wagon, so we'll take the ones we can find to hospital. I'll need your help, Patrick."

Patrick nodded. A bit of the bewilderment went out of his eyes now that he had something to do. He and

Duncan picked up Ernest and put him in the back of the wagon, then laid Winnie in beside him.

"I couldn't see any hurts on her," I told Duncan. "What's wrong with her?"

"I think she's injured inside," Duncan said. He hoisted me up next to Winnie. With some effort, Patrick heaved his bulk in after us.

"What about Mam?" I said. "Shouldn't she go with us?"

"I can only take the wounded this time around," Duncan said. "I'll come back for your mother. I promise."

I stared at him, aghast. I couldn't leave Mam to lay alone in the yard. Part of me wanted to scream my outrage, but I was too tired. I could barely hold up my head, I felt so weary now.

Duncan led the horse a little way along the road, and helped Mr. Neeson into the wagon. He bled from a deep cut in his head.

"She's gone, Rose," Mr. Neeson said. He held his broken fiddle in much the same manner that Catherine cradled her doll.

"Mrs. Neeson?" I asked.

"Aye. An awful thing. An awful thing. What could have caused it?" Mr. Neeson mumbled. He closed his eyes.

What could have caused it? Had it been German airships? Had it been the two ships that collided? Or had something else altogether caused the explosion? Something closer to me. A nudge at my mind. A secret. Deep inside. *Let me out!* No. I pushed it back down.

It was a slow, grisly journey. Duncan stopped frequently to clear the way of debris and bodies. The dead he left on the side of the road. The injured he placed in the delivery wagon. As the number of people in the wagon grew, the wooden floor became slippery with blood. The sharp metallic smell of it made me gag, so I tried to breathe through my mouth, only to have the dust and smoke that clogged the air choke me. I held Winnie's head in my lap. Her eyes were closed now, though occasionally her lips parted to let a moan escape. Patrick sat beside Ernest. He'd tried to take the binoculars, but Ernest clutched them to his chest with one hand. The other he used to tear at the makeshift bandage on his eyes, until Patrick grasped his fingers and held them inside his own.

Yellow flames spurted up on all sides of us. People probed and called and dug through the ruins of their homes with bare hands, desperate to rescue their families before fire claimed them. We wove our way past the orphanage, its walls demolished, and I remembered Bertie stopping to watch the boys toss a ball. Had it really been only yesterday? Where was Aunt Ida now? And Bertie? My mind pictured the kitchen stove toppling on him. I tried to stop the images but found I had no control over them.

A woman beside me called weakly for the priest. It suddenly dawned on me that Mam had had no priest to ease her passage into Heaven. And she was in Heaven, I told myself resolutely, extreme unction or not. We were the ones in Hell. I tried to block the woman's tormented cries from my ears, and closed my eyes, but even here there was no escape. Visions of fire and broken buildings haunted me.

We finally pulled up at Camp Hill Hospital. Chaos greeted us. Wagons, ambulances, motor cars, even wheelbarrows carried the injured. Nurses ran from one conveyance to another. One came to our wagon, a couple of soldiers accompanying her. She briefly held the wrist, then closed the eyes of the woman who had now stopped asking for the priest. She rolled Winnie's eyelids back, and raised Duncan's shirt from Ernest's head.

"These two in right away. Surgery," she ordered the soldiers. Winnie and Ernest disappeared into the hospital on stretchers.

"What hurts?" she asked me briskly.

"My arm's cut," I told her.

"And you, little girl?" she asked Catherine.

Catherine ignored the nurse, so after a moment I answered for her. "I think she got a bang on the head, but she's not said anything else hurts."

The nurse briefly parted Catherine's hair but didn't seem unduly alarmed. She turned to Patrick. "You?"

"My head hurts. Right by my ear," he said.

She ran her fingers over the side of his head. "You have glass in here, but nothing too serious. You three go in and wait in the hall. Someone will attend to you in time."

"What about Winnie and Ernest?" I asked. "They're my sister and brother."

"You'll see them later. Now go." She turned and went to a motor car.

Duncan came up. "I have to go back and get some more of the injured," he said. "They need anything that can move to transport people."

I clung to his arm. "No," I whispered. I knew no one else here but Patrick and Catherine, and I was scared.

He gently pried my fingers open. "I have to go, Rose. I'll come back and find you as soon as I can." He started away, then turned back. "Rose, was Mary at work today?"

I nodded. "She caught the morning car as usual."

"Good. I hope that means she was out of this."

I watched him climb into the wagon and leave, then followed Patrick and Catherine into the hospital.

We stopped inside the door, shocked at the number of people packed into the hallway. Some sat with their backs against the walls, others stretched full-length on the floor. Many were covered in the black rain like Patrick, and all had blood-soaked rags wrapped around various parts of their bodies. I recognized no one. A strange silence, broken by an occasional sob or moan, filled the corridor louder than any noise could. I wanted to turn and run away.

"Where do we go?" Catherine whispered. She gripped my cut arm, and I yelped.

"Out of the way." Two soldiers pushed past with a woman on a stretcher.

As I jumped aside, my knees buckled and I sank to the floor. Patrick and Catherine sat beside me, legs pulled up to their chins.

"We should have looked for my mama and granny and grandpa," Patrick said. He blinked rapidly several times and wiped his eyes on his sleeve. His left hand opened and shut convulsively, and I wondered if it was missing the bag of candy that was usually there.

I was exhausted but I fought sleep, terrified I might wake up in a worse nightmare than the one I was in. Instead, I scrutinized the faces of the injured for anyone I knew. Soldiers in khaki went by with boards and sheets to cover broken windows, while nurses in crisp white aprons floated like ghosts up and down the gloomy hall.

"I want my grandmother," Catherine suddenly announced.

"We could look around for her," Patrick suggested. "Mama and Dad might be here, too. And Granny and Grandpa."

It was too much effort to get up. I closed my eyes and pretended to sleep.

"Your father and Fred might be here." My eyes flew open. He was right. I still didn't know what had happened to Da and Fred or Mary. And where had Winnie and Ernest been taken? And what about Aunt Ida and Uncle James? Only yesterday Aunt Ida had told me I had such a large family it would take some doing to make me an orphan. I had to find out who had survived. I didn't want to be an orphan. I scrambled to my feet and started down the hall.

We stepped over people and peered into faces. Between the gloom of boarded windows and the black and battered faces, it was difficult to make out features—but not to make out the terrible injuries. I shrank from them at first, then made myself look. One of these people could be family.

Desperate, I searched inside myself for a prayer. *Our Father. . . .* But I could go no further. I felt nothing: no presence, no peace. He had left me, too. Well, I thought as I stared into yet another man's broken face, who needs You? Look what You've done.

But had He done this? Again, I had the suspicion of a secret hidden deep inside me. A horrible secret. One that threatened to come to the surface. One that could destroy me if released. *Let me out.* As before, I forced it down.

We went up a staircase to the second floor. Here, people lay unmoving in long rows of beds and mattresses crammed into every corner of a large room. The stench made Catherine gag. We stopped, none of us willing to go any farther.

"Are they dead?" Patrick asked.

"They're sleeping." A solidly built nurse came up behind us. She circled in front and blocked our view of the ward. "They've had surgery. You shouldn't be up here."

"My brother and sister. The nurse out front, she said they needed surgery. Are they here? Their names are Winnie and Ernest Dunlea." I tried to peer around her, but she stood her ground.

"I don't know most of these people's names and I don't have time to find out," the nurse said. "You need to go back downstairs." She herded us toward the staircase. "Wait." She gently lifted the doll blanket from my arm. Blood dripped from my fingertips. Seeing it made me suddenly woozy. "That needs looking after."

She pushed me back toward the ward. The floor tilted crazily. I leaned against the wall as beds whirled about me.

"What about you two?" she said to Patrick and Catherine. She examined Patrick's head. "That needs stitching, too, but not as badly as that girl's arm." She felt Catherine's head. "You're not too bad off. That cut just needs a dressing. You two go back downstairs."

"No!" Catherine shrieked. "I'm with her." She began to cry. "I have to stay with Rose." She darted past the nurse, grabbed my skirt and began to wail. I slid down the wall, sweat pouring off me. Catherine's voice echoed in my head.

"Stop that dreadful noise. You'll wake these people," the nurse scolded. "Very well. You can stay, but keep out of the way."

"I have to stay, too. I'm Rose's cousin," Patrick said. "I'm responsible for her."

I felt my dander go up at that. He wasn't responsible for me. Patrick didn't even like me. I wanted to tell the nurse that, but tiny black dots crowded my eyes. I shook my head to clear my vision. In a bed halfway down the ward was a face I knew. I had to reach it. I staggered to my feet, but the black dots floated together and a roar filled my ears.

I woke to find myself bundled in a cot with Catherine beside me. A soldier's greatcoat lay over us as a blanket. My arm burned. I probed it with my fingers and felt a bulky bandage. I had a dim memory of a man dressed in white bent over me, and a nurse holding my arm as a needle slipped in and out. I felt slightly ill remembering.

The black of the hospital ward was broken by sporadically spaced lamps. I could see a denser black through a gap where the blanket over the window beside me didn't quite reach the sill. Night had obviously fallen while I slept, though I had no idea how much time had passed.

Two women stood like shadows at the end of my

bed. They weren't nurses, as they were dressed in street clothes rather than white uniforms. One was slight— Mary's build. I struggled to sit up, but when the woman spoke her voice wasn't Mary's, so I lay back down and listened.

"I came to help out as soon as I heard," she said. A liquid, south Halifax voice. "These poor, poor people."

"The hospitals can't take any more. I heard they are sending some of the injured away to Truro and anywhere else that can take them in to be nursed," said the second woman. Her voice was older, more practical and definitely Richmond.

"How will these people ever get back on their feet?" said the first one. "Some of the things I've seen today, I never thought to see in all my life. One of the soldiers told me it was worse than anything he'd experienced in the war. And the children. So many of them left alone in the world."

"They'll manage. They'll have to," replied the first one, brusquely.

A powder of snow drifted through the gap. The older woman ran over and tucked the blanket securely around the window frame. She turned and caught me watching.

"You're awake," she whispered. "Do you need something for pain? I can get a nurse."

"No," I croaked. My tongue felt furry.

"A little water, then." The woman hurried off, and returned shortly with a glass of water, which she held to my lips.

"Your sister is very devoted to you." She smiled at the sleeping Catherine. "She insisted on staying with you the entire time the doctor fixed your arm."

I opened my mouth to tell her Catherine wasn't my sister. In fact, I wanted to tell the woman that Catherine made my life a daily misery, but a glance at the girl beside me held my tongue. What did it matter if they thought her my sister? Catherine didn't have anyone, and I hated to admit it, but neither did I. I raised my head and glanced around the ward. Was this the same one I'd fainted in? If so, I had to find that familiar face. I started to swing my legs over the bed, but the woman pushed them back beneath the greatcoat.

"Oh, no," she said. "Doctor said you were to stay right here tonight."

"But . . ." I protested. "I have to find . . ." I sank weakly back into the bed, too exhausted to speak. I'd search in the morning, I promised myself as sleep closed my eyes. I'd find him then.

Chapter 13

When next I opened my eyes, watery light filtered between the blanket and the window frame. Outside held the hushed feel of a snowfall—the snow Grandpa had predicted for Ernest and his sled.

Patrick materialized at the end of my bed, a bandage wrapped around his head. Enough of the black had been washed from his face to show purple half-moons beneath his eyes.

"They're sending the children to live with people away from Halifax," he said.

I sat upright, jolted my arm and grimaced at the pain. I put it out of my mind. I had more important things to think about right now. If I was sent away, I'd never find Da or Fred, and no one would be able to find me. I was the only one who knew where I was. Suddenly, I craned my neck to see up and down the hospital ward.

"Patrick, is this the same room I fainted in?" I asked urgently. I kept my voice low so as not to wake the people who slept.

"What?"

"Is this the same hospital room I fainted in yesterday?"

"I—I guess so." Patrick shrugged. "They all look the same to me."

"I saw Bertie here yesterday."

"Bertie?"

"I saw Bertie. In a bed. Halfway down the room," I insisted. I swung my legs over the side of the cot. My head swam momentarily, then cleared. I looked down to see myself fully dressed. The only things missing were my boots. I bent and saw them tucked under the bed. I pulled them on and quickly laced them up. It hurt to move my arm that much—hurt enough that the black dots crowded into my eyes again, but I blinked them away. No time to faint, I told myself. I took deep breaths to ward off waves of sickness.

"We have to go if we don't want to be sent away," I said.

"What about her?" Patrick pointed at Catherine.

I debated leaving her alone in the hospital bed. I'd be free of her, but strangely, I felt reluctant to do so.

"She can come with us," I said. I poked Catherine's arm. Sleepily, she pushed me away, so I prodded her harder.

"Why are you bringing her?" Patrick asked.

"She hasn't anyone else," I told him.

"What about her grandmother?"

"Get up!" I whispered in Catherine's ear.

Her eyes flew open and stared at me, confused.

"The children are being sent away to stay with

families outside Halifax. You can go with them if you want, but Patrick and I are leaving the hospital right now," I explained hurriedly. "You can come with us if you like." I realized it almost sounded like a plea. Two days ago, I would have been pleased to see the back side of Catherine, but now I wanted her to say she'd come.

Catherine felt around in the bed and pulled out her doll. Obviously she felt the same.

"Bring that soldier's coat," I whispered. "It's cold out and we'll need it."

Catherine wrapped the greatcoat around herself and the doll. Patrick headed for the door of the ward.

"Wait," I whispered. "I know I saw Bertie yesterday."

"He couldn't be here. Ernest said he was in the house near the stove. Duncan said he . . ." Patrick hesitated.

"I know what I saw," I said stubbornly. I turned away and walked down the room. People lay, some two to a bed as Catherine and I had been, others on the floor between, wrapped in blankets and coats. I carefully peered at each face.

"He's not here," Patrick said impatiently.

Desperate, I continued my search. "I know I saw him."

People stirred. Soon nurses would swarm in with bedpans and thermometers. I had to hurry. Then I was at the end of the room—and no Bertie. "Maybe it's the wrong floor," I said.

"He's dead, Rose."

I whirled on Patrick. "Don't say that. Don't you *ever* say that. I won't believe it until I see his body. This is the wrong floor. We'll have to check the others."

I stalked up the ward, then abruptly stopped. Another face, not as familiar, but still one I recognized. I turned back, and a man's feverish eyes watched me approach.

"I remember you from the dock, girl," he said. "Bringing your brother's lunch, wasn't it?"

I nodded. That's where I'd seen him before. He worked with Da.

"One of Michael Dunlea's brood, right?"

I nodded again. I opened my mouth, then snapped it shut. If I asked the question then I'd know the answer, and I'd never not know it again.

Somehow, I found the courage. *Did you see my Da?* I mouthed the words, unable to speak them aloud.

"What's that?" The man shifted restlessly in the bed.

I licked my dry lips. "Did you see my Da? Or Fred? My brother, Fred Dunlea?" I didn't need to tell the man *when* I meant.

He shook his head. "I was behind a boxcar. It shielded me from the blast somewhat, though I still lost this—" He gestured down at the bed, and I saw the sheets flat where his left leg should have been.

"Last I saw, your dad and brother were stacking supplies on the dock. The one nearest the burning ships.

They couldn't have lived through that explosion, girl. I'm sorry."

"But you're alive," I protested. "Maybe . . ."

The man pressed his lips together and shook his head.

"But maybe . . ."

He looked away from me.

No! I don't know if I screamed aloud or not, though the word vibrated resoundingly inside my head. *No!* Not Da. Not Fred. I felt myself pulled down a dark tunnel, around twists and turns, toward an even greater black. *There's comfort here*, it promised. *The cries, the wails, the broken bodies, the pain in your heart, they're not here. You can stay forever in this dark place—no thoughts to torture you, no grief to tear you apart.*

Fingers wrapped around my upper arm and white hot pain shot through me. Patrick immediately dropped his hand from my elbow.

"Sorry," he muttered quickly. "I forgot about your cut."

I dashed tears from my eyes and rounded on him, ready to lash out—but stopped. He'd brought me back from that dark place.

With Catherine following, we walked quickly toward the door of the ward. As we reached it, a nurse in a starched white uniform covered by a navy wool cape stopped us. "Where do you children think you're going?" she asked.

"We're going to find our families," I told her.

"There's a blizzard starting. Outside is no place for you now." She began to herd us back into the room.

"No." It was difficult to stand up to her. I could hear Mam's voice in my ear telling me to be polite to my elders, but this was one time I would disobey her. "We're going to find our families," I repeated to the nurse, my voice shaking. "We're the only ones left who can."

"Some people have offered their homes to children like you who are left alone. Only until your families are located and come for you," the nurse said.

"But what if they never come?" I asked.

She stared at me for several moments. "Well, you can't go out like that."

I planted my feet firmly, ready to do battle.

The nurse undid a clasp at her neck and took off the cape. She wrapped it around me. "That will keep you warm," she said, briskly.

"I'll return it," I promised.

She nodded. She picked up a couple of towels from a tray and tied them around my head and Catherine's to cover our ears. "Don't want to add frostbite to all your problems."

"My brother Ernest and my sister Winnie were brought here," I said. "Do you know where they are?"

The nurse shook her head. "So many people have been brought in. There's a list being compiled downstairs of everyone in the hospital, though it'll take a while to draw up. You might want to check. Also, downstairs they are handing out cups of hot soup. You each have one before you go out—you hear?"

We nodded.

"There was a little boy yesterday . . . four years old . . . in a bed halfway down . . . red hair," I said haltingly. Had I wanted to find Bertie so bad that my mind had made him up?

"I don't know, dear. So many—" A second nurse called to her and she made to move away. "I must go. You children take care." She turned back. "I hope you find them, and God bless."

I didn't want God's blessing. I was angry that He had let this horrible thing happen to us. But mostly I was scared. Scared that if I asked Him why, this time He might answer. And my secret would get out.

Before we went downstairs, I led Patrick and Catherine on a grim tour of the rest of the hospital. Tucked in a bed in a corner of a ward, we found Ernest, eyes bandaged.

"Ernest." I put a hand on his leg and shook it, but he didn't stir.

"Been like that all night, poor tyke. Never saw him move once." A woman in the bed next to him propped herself on her elbows to speak. "You family?"

I nodded.

"Lost an eye, I heard."

Stunned, I stared at her in disbelief, then turned and started to leave.

"Is there a message for him?" the woman called after me.

I stopped. "Tell him—" My mind reeled. What was there *to* say? I shook my head and left. I continued my search, but could not find Winnie or Bertie. I saw a couple of girls from school, and three women from our church, but no one else from our family, nor Catherine's grandmother.

We went downstairs to the main floor. Confusion still reigned, but it had an ordered air about it this time. People milled about a desk. I pushed through and saw two women with a sheaf of papers in front of them. One wrote frantically, while the other leafed through the pages.

A man elbowed me aside, enveloping me in the sour smell of wet wool. Snow melted in his hair. "Is my wife here? My children? Katherine Black? Anyone by the name Black?" he asked.

The woman ran a finger down a page, flipped it over and continued her search on a second one. "I have no one named Black."

"They must be here," he insisted. "I've been to the other hospitals. This is the only one left."

"I'm sorry," she said. "The army has set up a tent city on the Common. There were people there overnight. Plus, many people took shelter in private homes. There's also a temporary morgue set up in Chebucto Road School. You could try there."

My mouth dropped open at her mention of the morgue. She had as good as told this man that his family might be dead. Then I saw the distress in the woman's eyes and realized she had only done what she had to do.

The man's shoulders slumped and he stumbled back through the crowd. I squeezed into the space left.

"Dunlea?" I asked. "Anyone named Dunlea? D–U–N–L–A–E."

"That's not how you spell it," Patrick snapped. "Don't you even know how to spell your own name!" He turned to the woman. "Don't mind her, she's slow. D–U–N–L–E–A. And my parents are named Murphy. M–U–R–P–H–Y."

The woman went quickly down her list. "There's no one here by that name. But there are a lot of people in the hospital whose names we don't know. They haven't been able to tell us, or they've been in surgery and are unconscious still."

"Rose?"

I turned to see Sister Therese smiling shakily at me. Dried blood stained the front of her habit and a bandage was wrapped around her forehead, its white melting into that of her wimple.

"I'm so glad to see you're safe," she said. "I want to

thank you for helping the girls get out of the school."

"Mam's dead," I said flatly. I needed to say those words, feel them on my tongue, see if they felt true. They did.

"I'm so sorry, dear," she said. She hugged me.

"And Catherine. How are you?"

"I'm fine, Sister," she said. "Have you seen my grandmother?"

Sister Therese shook her head. "She might be here. It's so chaotic. People come and go. I can't keep track of them. I came down to help out wherever needed."

"What happened to the other girls?" I asked. "And Sister Frances?" I surprised myself by my concern for the teacher.

"Many of the students were hurt. Some were killed. We don't know how many." Sister Therese blinked rapidly. "Sister Frances suffered cuts and bruises like most of us, but she'll be fine. The school is destroyed. I'm not sure what will happen—if it will be rebuilt or torn down. But there won't be school for you children for a long time."

No school. The secret hammered at my brain to be revealed. I winced from the pain it shot through my head, but I would not let it out.

"We're going to find our families," I told Sister Therese.

She frowned, and I got myself ready to run if she wanted to keep us there.

"Yes. You go look for your families. I trust you, Rose."

She fumbled inside her sleeve, pulled out an object and pressed it into my hands. "This is for you. To help you in your search and keep you safe."

I looked down to see a rosary. Sister Therese folded my fingers over the beads.

"I'll keep you all in my prayers," she said.

Patrick looked relieved. I wished I could feel the same comfort that I was being kept in Sister Therese's prayers, but there was none. The beads felt hard and cold and lifeless to my touch. I pushed the rosary deep into the pocket of my dress. Sister Therese directed us toward the soup kitchen, then disappeared.

As I sat in the kitchen a few minutes later, fingers wrapped around a hot cup, I vowed I'd find my family if I had to search every hospital and nursing home, the tent city, and even—I shuddered—the Chebucto Road School morgue.

Chapter 14

Bitterly cold wind threw hard snow pellets into my face as I stepped out the hospital door. I pulled the nurse's cape tight about my shoulders. Motor cars and wagons continued to pull up with wounded. A party of soldiers, shovels in hand, moved off at a quick march to dig through the ruins. The faces of everyone around us were drawn and haggard, eyes haunted. I glanced at Patrick and Catherine and saw they looked the same. I probably did, too. We stood a moment, trying to decide where to go first. Then, of their own accord, my feet started off in the direction of home. I needed to see if Mam still lay in our backyard, or whether Duncan had taken her away as he had promised.

Snowdrifts piled up against the rubble, softening the starkness of the devastation. Wind swept unchecked over the newly flattened land, fanning the fires that still smouldered. I recognized nothing, but my feet moved surely, the way engraved in my mind. Again, I was surprised at the silence broken only by the occasional shout from rescue workers, but by none of the spare words we used in everyday life. We passed the ruins of shops, including the sweet store, Patrick's favourite. My feet grew numb in the cold and my hands clasped beneath the cape for warmth. Catherine staggered along, the soldier's greatcoat tangled about her feet. She kept up a running conversation with her doll, of tea parties and new dresses and her father.

"Do you think your father will come home from Europe now?" I asked Catherine.

She lowered her head and tucked the doll within her coat sleeve. "I don't know."

"I'm sure they'll let him out of the army if they know you are alone," I continued.

Catherine merely shrugged, and the conversation ended.

We arrived at a church and went in. Part of one wall had collapsed, but it was dry and women bustled about with soup and bread. I took a cup, but the thought of food gagged me so I merely held it to warm my hands. Patrick gulped his down, while Catherine sipped daintily, then offered some to her doll. I averted my eyes from the cross at the front of the church and studied the people. I wished that Aunt Ida or Mary was among them. I wished so hard that it was a disappointment when neither of them appeared.

We left the church and continued walking in the direction of home. The smoke became thicker. Ash filled our throats and an acrid stench stung our nostrils.

I pulled the cape over my nose and breathed in the faint scent of perfume left by the nurse. Mam had always smelled nice, too.

"You can't go any farther." A soldier with a gun barred our way. "Only rescue workers allowed to pass."

"But we live here," I said.

"No one is allowed in but rescue workers," he repeated.

Patrick elbowed me aside and faced the soldier. "Our houses are here. We want to go home."

"No one has a house here anymore. There's nothing left. It's too dangerous to let you roam about. Sorry, sonny," the soldier said, unbending slightly from his stiff stance.

Patrick blustered about for a moment, then sagged with defeat.

"What do we do now?" he asked me.

"We'll check the tent city and Victoria General Hospital and anywhere else they took injured people," I said. I needed to keep moving to keep the secret controlled. It clamoured to be set free among these ruins.

Rows of tents had been placed on the Common, but without heat, the blizzard made them uninhabitable. People huddled in groups around bonfires. I scrutinized each face, and recognized a neighbour or two, but they were few and far between. Suddenly, it came to me why. Most of our neighbours were dead. I tore my thoughts away from that path. If I started to think about it, I would cry and never stop. I warmed my hands by a fire and listened to two men talk about the disaster.

"It was those two ships on fire in the Narrows," one man said to the other. "The *Imo* and the *Mont Blanc*. Loaded with explosives that one was."

I had seen both those vessels through Ernest's binoculars.

"I still think it was the Germans. Sabotage," said the other.

I moved away, not wanting to hear any more.

We searched all day in the driving snow, from hospitals to hastily erected shelters where the wounded were treated. Lists of injured were being posted now, and Patrick would grandly sweep me aside any time we came across one to read the names himself. At first it made me furious that he did, but I had to admit, he could go through the lists faster than I was able to. We stopped everyone and asked if they'd seen Da, Fred, Mary, Uncle James, Aunt Ida, Aunt Helen, Uncle Lyle, Granny and Grandpa. Patiently, we recited their names again and again. Always the answer was no. I got to the point where I didn't have the heart to ask anymore.

Dusk had gathered when Catherine plopped down on a snow-covered pile of boards and refused to go any farther. "Dolly and I are cold," she stated through chattering teeth.

Wind howled and whistled about the ruins, pushing sheets of snow before it. At times we waded over our

knees through drifts. Like Catherine I shivered uncontrollably. The bumps and bruises I'd received the day
before were making themselves known and my stitched
arm throbbed. But there was one last place we needed
to check.

"We'll get a hot drink soon, Catherine," I assured
her. I pulled her to her feet. Dried tear trails stained her
cheeks. I put a hand to my own face and felt the stiff-
ness there. I'd been crying, too. Strange to not have
known.

I held Catherine's hand, conjured up the map in my
mind and set off to Chebucto Road School, now the
mortuary.

Snow caked our hair and eyelids by the time we
arrived. We stepped indoors, grateful to be out of the
wind, though our breath still puffed white. One wall
sagged, but it had been shored up and the windows
covered with boards. The gloom was broken by pools
of yellow light from lamps. A wagon pulled up at the
door behind us, and I averted my eyes from the blan-
keted bulges stacked in its back.

Soldiers came and went, their faces weary. People
stood huddled in small groups, but here, too, was that
eerie silence that haunted the entire city. Three soldiers
sat at a table, sorting watches, rings, papers, clothing,
books, lunch pails and school bags. Occasionally, one
would sweep a pile into a cloth bag, tie and label it, then
set it aside. Two more soldiers and a man in a suit and

bowler hat sat at a second table. A woman clutched a baby, and leaned over the table to watch anxiously as the man in the suit read from a paper in his hand. Her body trembled, but from cold or fear I didn't know. The man whispered to one of the soldiers standing nearby.

"This way, Missus," he said, and led her to a flight of stairs leading downward. They disappeared from sight.

"Scared the wits out of me," I heard a voice behind me say. I turned to see two soldiers in the doorway of the school. They lit cigarettes and tossed the used matches into the storm. "You think they're all dead down there," one said. "And suddenly this body sits up and lets out a yell. Made my blood curdle, it being the middle of the night and all."

The second soldier nodded. "The number of people we brought in yesterday. Easy to see how a live one could be thought for dead if they were knocked out."

"A boy it was, about thirteen," the first went on. "Leg sheared off at the knee." He glanced up and saw me, then lowered his voice.

I strained to make out his words, fascinated and repulsed at the same time.

"How that boy lived so long with one leg is beyond me. Probably no family left. Might have been better if he'd never woken up." The first soldier threw away his cigarette end. "Better get back to work." They began to unload the wagon of its gruesome cargo.

"Can I help you, children?" The man in the suit asked.

I'd not noticed that we'd moved to the front of the line. "We're looking for our families," I said.

For being so cold a moment ago, I suddenly felt faint with heat.

"You're too young to go into the morgue to identify people," he said.

"But we're the only ones left in our family," I told him flatly.

He looked taken aback. He shuffled papers in front of him, hummed and hawed, then cleared his throat. "You're still too young."

"I'm fourteen," I said. I was near enough that I didn't think that counted as a lie.

"I'm sixteen," Patrick chimed in.

I turned and glared at him. No one would believe Patrick was sixteen. His voice hadn't even lowered and his chin hadn't sprouted a single hair.

The man raised his eyebrows at Patrick, but didn't argue. "Who are you looking for?" he asked. He signalled to the soldier beside him to write the information down.

I went through my list of names. They came easily off my tongue now, I'd repeated them so often.

The soldier's pen hovered over the paper. "That many missing?" he said softly. "I'm so sorry, miss."

It wasn't until then that it hit me. *That many?* I felt like I'd been punched in the stomach.

"Get a chair for the young lady," the man in the suit ordered.

"I'm fine," I said. I took a deep breath.

"Give us those names again, please. One at a time, along with their age and appearance."

I described Frederick first. The man in the suit went through a list and put a tick beside some numbers. I could barely read words right side up in front of me, so words written upside down were next to impossible, but I guessed the list was a description of everyone brought to the mortuary. The check marks showed those who possibly matched my description. When I got to Bertie, I hesitated. I didn't want them to match Bertie with anyone on that list. Reluctantly, I described him. Finished, I stepped aside for Catherine. She ignored us and chatted to her doll, so I told them about her grandmother as best I could. Patrick went next, then the man in the suit nodded, and a soldier stood up.

"This way, girls. You too, son."

"I don't think Catherine should come," I said. I'd felt a growing concern about her behaviour. We were the same age, but she was acting so much younger right now. Younger even than Winnie. "I'll look for her grandmother for her."

The soldier nodded, then led Patrick and me to the

top of the stairs. Patrick's eyes darted every which way. Sweat trickled down the sides of his face and he looked decidedly green. I knew how he felt. I'd not seen many people passed away, my Mam's mother being the closest to us. Laid out in her best dress in a coffin in our parlour, she'd looked like she was sleeping peacefully. I didn't know what I'd see here, but I knew it wasn't going to be like that. I steeled myself to go down.

Suddenly, I felt myself turned about and swept into a huge embrace. "Rose, oh, Rose. I've been looking for you everywhere . . ."

My sister Mary held me so tight, I couldn't breathe. Her fingers were white with cold, her dress shoes soaked and falling apart. A second person came up and pulled me from Mary into another hug. Aunt Ida. I clung to her. Like so many others I'd seen this day, her head sported a white dressing. Duncan loomed behind them, face pale with fatigue.

"You didn't come back," I accused him.

"I did," he said. "You were sleeping with Catherine in the hospital. I didn't want to wake you. I had to go back out and help bring in more wounded. I've been working all night and day."

The anger drained out of me. Duncan had kept his word. I shouldn't have doubted him.

"Where's Horace?" I asked Mary. Strange that question should be the first in my head.

"*Horse* is at his house lamenting the fact that the army

took his beloved car to use as an ambulance." Mary laughed bitterly. "I asked him to bring me home when I heard about the explosion, but he said he was too busy. Didn't want to get his hands dirty, he meant. I made my way to Richmond on my own, though it took me until late yesterday afternoon."

Suddenly I remembered. "Mam's dead, Mary. In the backyard."

"Duncan told me. He brought her here." Tears washed down Mary's face.

"I'm sorry you had to see your mother like that, Rose," Aunt Ida said.

"But at least I know she's dead," I told her. "Ernest and Winnie were at the hospital with us, but I could only find Ernest when I went to find them this morning. A woman told me he'd lost an eye. I don't know where Winnie is. I can't find Da or Fred or Bertie. And I couldn't find you or Mary—"

"Hush, hush." Aunt Ida patted my back. "I spent the night at Victoria Hospital from this bump on the head. That's where Mary found me. We set out this morning and came across Duncan. He told us you were at the Camp Hill hospital. We went there straight away, but you had already left. We saw Ernest."

"What about Winnie?" I asked through chattering teeth.

"She's had an operation," Aunt Ida said.

An operation! I had heard Granny talk about people

who had an operation. They generally died. I gripped
Aunt Ida's arm tightly.

"The doctor said she'd be fine in time," Aunt Ida
hastily assured me. "Her spleen, an organ inside, was
torn. They fixed it. She was sent by train to Truro as
they felt she'd get better care there."

The soldier shifted impatiently. Others waited to go
down the stairs.

"You don't need to go, Rose. I can look," Aunt Ida
said.

I shook my head. I had come this far. "I need to see
for myself."

"Very well, then." She nodded at the soldier to lead
us down.

"I don't want to go," Patrick said suddenly. He
backed away.

At the bottom of the stairs, Aunt Ida gasped and
crossed herself. Row upon row of covered bodies was
laid out. I couldn't believe there were so many. Mary
crowded close behind, Duncan's arm about her
shoulder.

"I'll just show you the people who most closely
match the descriptions the young miss gave us,
ma'am," the soldier said. "Some of them aren't in very
good shape. Just so you know."

Ice reached into my bones and wrapped around my
heart, squeezing it until I could barely breathe. Electric
lights had been strung up—probably the only ones in

all of Richmond. They cast ghostly shadows across the walls. It was a horrible place. The soldier went along the rows reading each tag. Occasionally he would stop and gently lift the cotton from a face. I buried my head in Aunt Ida's coat. She would let me know if anyone was found.

Mary gave a small moan.

"Yes," Aunt Ida said. "That's Mrs. Murphy. Helen Murphy. The boy's mother."

Farther along the line. "Mrs. Dunlea, the elder. Rose's grandmother," Aunt Ida said gently.

We found Grandpa, and Mam. She had a tag that said *Alice Mary Dunlea*. We couldn't find Uncle Lyle, Da, Fred or Bertie.

"Also—" Aunt Ida's voice broke. "My husband, James Dunlea, is missing." She described what he had worn to work, his age, and the fact that he was a steve-dore on the docks.

"A lot of workers on the docks just disappeared. We haven't had many come in from the waterfront," the soldier said. "A tidal wave formed after the explosion and swept across the docks and the lower part of town, washing people into the ocean. And . . ." He hesitated. "Some of the bodies here are badly burnt. We won't ever know who they were. But come back and check again. More people are brought in all the time."

"Thank you," Aunt Ida said. "It's not an easy job you have, but you're doing it well."

I looked up to see the soldier's face crumble at her words. He struggled to compose himself. I had thought of him just as a soldier in uniform, but I now realized he was a boy barely older than Frederick. He'd never seen battle or death until now.

Duncan followed us up the stairs. "Tomorrow we'll search the hospitals again. But right now, I'm taking you to my mother's. There're no windows left in the house, but the building is still sound and there are beds. I think the best thing for you all is to get some rest."

Aunt Ida nodded, and we climbed into the milk wagon and made our way slowly through the ruins.

Chapter 15

As Duncan had said, his house still stood, though one wall on the second storey had a jagged hole in it.

"A large chunk of metal from the ship tore right through that," Duncan's father exclaimed. High on a ladder, he hammered a final nail into a board over a window, then climbed down. "Imagine, a piece of the ship being blown over half a mile into my upstairs bedroom."

Duncan's mother was in the back porch. She fed wood into an old stove. A new gas range stood proudly in the kitchen, but as the gas was cut off, the range didn't work. "It's a good thing I kept this old stove back here," she said. She heated water to wash our faces and warmed bricks to place in our beds.

Two mattresses were dragged into the corner of the kitchen nearest the porch. Patrick took one, and Catherine and I the other. She instantly fell asleep. I watched her for a few minutes, the way she clutched the doll even in her exhaustion. Where was the sharp-tongued Catherine? She had followed me meekly all day, her words kept for the doll. Despite all that had happened, Catherine's behaviour unsettled me the most.

I lay back, but my brain wouldn't stop. It wanted to go over every wrecked building, every ruined body, every wretched detail, again and again. Bertie. Had I really seen him in the hospital? I was so sure, but Mary and Aunt Ida both said they hadn't come across him when they'd searched for us.

A piece of wood cracked loudly in the stove, and I jumped, my heart thudding.

"It's nothing, Rose," Aunt Ida said. "Get some rest."

I lay back down and stretched my feet toward the warm brick, but couldn't relax. I listened to Aunt Ida, Duncan and his parents talking.

"It was the Germans who did it," Mr. MacDonald said. "Sabotage. They set that fire on board the ship."

The secret pushed insistently at me.

"I think it was an accident," Aunt Ida said. "The ships collided. I heard the *Mont Blanc* had munitions on board, TNT, explosives. That's what caused it."

"I heard they both had a clear lane in the harbour. How could they run into each other?" Mrs. MacDonald exclaimed.

"I guess someone made a mistake," Aunt Ida said.

"I heard the police are rounding up all the Germans," Duncan added. "People want them arrested until they know who did it."

"That's not right," Aunt Ida protested.

"Maybe not, but that's what they're doing."

Until they know who did it.

Abruptly, I fell into a darkness that, mercifully, carried no dreams.

For the next two days I only opened my eyes to have a little tea and bread and use the chamber pot, before I fell asleep again. I was aware of people about me—Catherine sharing the mattress, food cooked, the stove stoked, voices—but I didn't want to be part of that world anymore, so I kept my eyes closed.

"She's exhausted," I heard Aunt Ida say. "Let her sleep. It'll help her arm to heal faster."

The morning of the third day, Aunt Ida shook my shoulder and wouldn't stop until I pried open my eyes.

"Rose, you have to get up now. You've slept enough."

I shook my head. With the windows all boarded up, the kitchen was sunk in permanent gloom. I could pretend it was still night.

"Yes, Rose," she insisted.

It was safe here, inside sleep where there were no thoughts, no pain, no heartache and no secret.

"Rose," Aunt Ida said firmly, "you have to wake up."

I opened my eyes, and the secret exploded into my brain. I knew who had caused the explosion. *Please, God, make it so I don't have to go to school.* I had asked and He had answered. But I couldn't let anyone else know. I couldn't stand it if no one loved me anymore. I'd lost so much already.

I choked down a glass of milk, while Catherine

toasted me a slice of bread. I picked at it, but my throat closed.

"I can't eat it," I told Aunt Ida.

"Never mind. Perhaps later," she said.

Patrick brought in an armful of wood for Mrs. Mac-Donald. He appeared thinner, his cheeks hollow. Aunt Ida shooed him from the kitchen and filled a tin tub with warm water. She helped me into it. I felt shaky, like I'd been ill for a long time.

Aunt Ida peeled back the bandage from my arm and examined the cut. "It's looking quite good," she announced with satisfaction. "I'll take you to a nursing station in a few days to get those stitches taken out."

"Where's Mary?" I asked. I made my sentences short, afraid the secret would fly from my tongue.

"She's gone to the relief office to see about a place for us to stay for a while. I'm not sure how she will do."

"Now, there's no hurry," Mrs. McDonald protested.

"You've been so good to us, but we can't stay indefinitely," Aunt Ida said. She lathered my hair gently with soap, then exclaimed over a piece of glass she had to pull from my head. "Duncan is still helping with the rescue. He's not had a moment's rest."

"He's ferrying around the big American doctors," Mrs. MacDonald put in proudly.

"Yes, Rose. The city of Boston sent us trainloads of medical supplies and doctors and nurses. They've truly been wonderful to us. Shipments of window glass are on their way. Everyone in Canada and the United States is helping. An American eye doctor is examining Ernest later today. Eventually they'll fit him for a glass eye." Her voice broke momentarily.

"At least there's no shortage of food or clothing now that things are organized," Duncan's mother said. "I'll send Patrick and Catherine down to get us some groceries, though she isn't much use that one. Doesn't know her way around a kitchen. I doubt she has ever boiled a pot of water!"

I climbed from the tub and dried myself in front of the stove. It didn't seem possible, but my legs and arms looked skinnier than ever.

"Her grandmother had a maid," I said. *Just like I was going to be, a million years ago.*

Aunt Ida gently pulled a comb through my tangles, stopping now and then to work a piece of glass from my scalp. "Your hair dries quickly," she said. "I envy you. It takes me all day to dry mine." She turned me around and looked me over. "Now, there's the girl I know." She tried to smile but her lips quivered. Such haunted eyes, filled with the loss of Uncle James and the others. Ashamed, I lowered my own. I knew who had done this to her. Suddenly, she pulled me to her, and I felt her shoulders heave. After a moment, she let me go and dabbed at her eyes with the towel.

"Look at me, now, going all to pieces. Sorry, Rose. Lately, it just takes me unawares.

"I'm going to see Ernest this morning, if you'd like to come with me," she went on. "I took the train to Truro to see Winnie yesterday. The doctor says she's doing well, though she does look very peaky. She asked if you could come next time and tell her stories. About the Irish Chain quilt, she said.

"I also saw Sister Therese, who said you must be sure to stop by and visit her when you go to see Ernest. She's lending a hand at the hospital. She also said that you were quite a heroine. She says you saved a lot of girls' lives. I told her it was only what we would expect you to do."

"I'm still a bit tired," I lied. "I think I'll stay here. Or I could help Patrick get the groceries, and get some fresh air. That would be good for me, the fresh air," I added desperately. I couldn't face Ernest and his wrecked eye. And how could I tell Winnie stories about the Irish Chain quilt? No doubt it had burned in the fire, and besides, I no longer had the right to tell stories of brave Great-grandmother Rose. I had destroyed our house, killed Da, Fred, Mam, Uncle James, Granny and Grandpa, and Patrick's parents, and put Ernest and Winnie in the hospital. And lost Bertie. And I didn't have the gumption to tell anyone. My legs and arms trembled violently. Aunt Ida made a move toward me, but I quickly bent to tidy the bed, and she held back.

"Perhaps it's for the best. You need time to recover," she said after a moment.

Duncan's mother handed me a list of what to ask for at the food depot. "If you look in the back porch, you'll find an old sled of Duncan's to use to bring the parcels home, though I understand it's more ice than snow out there today. First a blizzard, then an ice storm, though it's hard to tell what is going on with the windows all boarded up. I'll be glad to get glass and get things back to normal."

Normal. I no longer knew what normal was, but I nodded, draping the nurse's cape over my shoulders and fastening the clasp. As I did, I realized I would have to go back to the hospital to return it. Maybe I could sneak in and out without anyone noticing me.

"Rose, see if you can find a coat to fit you at the depot," Aunt Ida said, echoing my thoughts. "A black or dark coat," she added.

For mourning, I knew.

"And, I guess, anything else you can find to fit yourself, Winnie and the boys, or rather, Ernest . . ." Her voice trailed off. "I don't know what to tell you to get," she suddenly cried. "There's nothing left, and I don't know what you need." She buried her face in her hands. A tremor of unease went through me. What would happen to us if Aunt Ida got sick? What if she couldn't take care of us? We'd have to go to an orphanage.

Mrs. MacDonald put an arm around Aunt Ida's shoulders. "There, there, dear. Hard times, but it'll get better."

"It couldn't get much worse, could it?" Aunt Ida said. She fought to steady her voice. "Get some underclothes for yourself and Catherine. Stockings. A couple of night-gowns. If you give me the list, I'll write what to get."

I handed the list to her and went to the back porch to find the sled. I wiped cobwebs from the runners, then went back in to get the list. Paper in hand, I dragged the sled down the porch steps to where Catherine and Patrick waited.

"Why don't you leave the doll here," I said to Catherine. For some reason, seeing her cradle the toy so tenderly made me mad.

Catherine's eyes widened in surprise at my sharp tone. "I have to take care of her," she said. She tucked the doll into the crook of her arm.

Patrick snatched the paper out of my hand. "What's this?" he asked.

"It's a list Mrs. MacDonald gave to me of things to get." I tried to grab it back, but he held it out of reach.

"Why did she give it to you?" he asked scornfully. "You can't read it. You're simple."

He was right back to being hateful Patrick. I lunged at him and wrapped my arms around his legs, and we fell over in a heap. I began to hit him with my fists. He protected his head with upraised arms and started yelling. Catherine stood in one spot and shrieked loudly, but I kept pounding away. My arm hurt fiercely, but I couldn't stop myself.

"Stop! Stop it, Rose." Aunt Ida ran down the porch steps. "You'll open that cut again."

Strong arms lifted me off Patrick and held me tight. I began to scream—

"Stop that racket right now," a man's voice ordered.

Every muscle in my body froze solid as if I'd been dipped in water and left out in the cold. I couldn't move. Neither could anyone else: Aunt Ida stared with wide eyes, Patrick lay motionless on the ground where I'd toppled him, Catherine's last shriek echoed in the crisp air, then died away.

"That's better." The arms let me go.

I turned to see Uncle James.

Aunt Ida melted first. She moaned, then put a hand to her mouth. "What are you doing here?" Tears spilled over her cheeks.

Uncle James swept her into a big hug. Patrick scrambled to his feet and ran over to him, but I took a step backward. A ghost?

Uncle James turned to me. "Rose? Don't I get a hug?"

I shook my head. If I touched him, he'd disappear again, like smoke or mist—like Da or Fred.

Aunt Ida's hand clasped in his, Uncle James knelt in front of me. "I'm real," he assured me.

I threw my arms around his neck. He was real.

"Tell me why you were beating up Patrick. Your Mam wouldn't be pleased to see you fighting a boy."

"Mam's dead," I said shortly.

"Dead?" Uncle James repeated. He picked me up like I was Bertie.

"Come in where it's warm," Aunt Ida said. She clutched his coat. I doubted she'd ever let go of him again. We all crowded into the kitchen. Uncle James set me on a chair at the table.

"Bless me. Bless me." Mrs. MacDonald bustled to the stove and put on the kettle. "Bless me. Bless me."

"I looked for you everywhere," Aunt Ida said. Her eyes never left his face. I knew she was afraid he'd vanish.

"The force of the explosion carried me away," he said. "I got a terrific whack on the head, almost split it open, but I have a strong skull." He rapped his head.

I knew he was trying to make light of his injury to save Aunt Ida any distress.

"I lost my memory for a while. I was told I was found wandering around near Rockhead Prison. I still don't remember that part at all. They'd made a sort of hospital there at the prison, and they kept me in bed for a couple of days. Finally, this morning, I remembered who I was. I went home looking for you, Ida. Not much left of it, is there. Nothing left at all of Michael's or the old folks' places. I was setting out to search the hospitals, when I met Mr. Neeson. He told me he heard you were staying here with the MacDonalds." He reached out and gripped Aunt Ida's hand. "I was awful glad to hear you were safe," he said gruffly. "I've been sick with worry."

My mind had been working the whole time he talked. "But you were on the docks like Da and Fred . . ." I began excitedly.

"No. Fred and Michael and Lyle—they were all at the waterfront loading ships. I was on the night shift, so I was finished work and on my way home. I stopped to watch the ships burn with the others, then decided I needed my bed more. I was a good piece away from the docks when the explosion happened. Probably the only thing that saved me. No one at the waterfront could have survived. No one. They wouldn't have felt a thing, Rose, it happened so fast." His shoulders slumped and I saw how tired his face was. Aunt Ida saw it, too.

"I'll get you a cup of tea. Warm you up," she said.

"Who's left, then?" Uncle James asked quietly.

"Well, these two you can see in front of you. Bruises and bumps, but they'll do," Aunt Ida said. "Ernest is in the hospital; he lost an eye. Winnie was badly hurt; she had an operation, but she's coming along fine. She's in hospital in Truro. Mary's at the relief office seeing about a place for us to stay."

"That's all?" said Uncle James after a moment.

Aunt Ida bit her lip and nodded. "Your folks are at the Chebucto Road School. They've made it into a mortuary. We found them there. Alice and Helen, also."

"And I saw Bertie at the hospital," I announced.

"Oh, Rose," Aunt Ida said.

"I did," I said stubbornly. "I saw him in a bed halfway down the ward."

"You were fainting," Patrick jeered. "You couldn't see anything."

"I saw him."

"What were you two fighting about when I came up?" Uncle James asked in an attempt to stave off a new argument.

"He grabbed a list of supplies Mrs. MacDonald gave to me to take to the relief depot!" I said heatedly.

"You can't even read, so what's the point of you having the list?" Patrick argued.

"Because it was given to me!"

"Give her back the list," Uncle James ordered. "And you both go and get the supplies."

"She's slow, Uncle James. She can't even read it. It'll take forever to get everything," Patrick whined.

"That's why I hit him. Because he said I'm slow."

I *was* slow. Simple. Retarded. All those words Sister Frances, Patrick and Catherine threw out at me. And because I was slow, I had caused the explosion. I hated Patrick, but mostly I hated myself.

Chapter 16

We bunched in a small group around the open grave, its black soil piled high against the white snow. In the pine box next to the hole was Mam. There was no laying out of the body in a parlour, no church in which to have a funeral Mass; there were no songs, no stories told. When Mam's mother died the house had been full of people. Stories were told about Grandma. Mam said stories were memories, a way to hold on to lost ones.

There were so many dead to be buried, Father McManus spent his days at the cemetery. While he intoned the solemn words, the sound of shovels rang on frozen ground, the soldiers hard-pressed to dig the many graves needed.

Wind swirled about my legs, but I didn't feel the cold. The undertakers' helpers did, though. They shifted from foot to foot, anxious to get the service over so they could snatch a moment of warmth before the next burial. Undertakers had come from as far as Toronto to help bury our dead. Two soldiers stood quietly nearby, hats in hands, shovels at their feet. They would cover Mam up after we left. I noticed all this because I didn't want to look at the pine box.

An extra hard gust of wind threatened to wrench away Aunt Ida's hat, and we crowded closer together. Yet another blizzard had swept down on Halifax, further hampering the rescue efforts. Except there wasn't anyone left to rescue. Only the dead to find.

Father McManus rushed the last words of the service. The box was lowered into the hole by the undertakers and soldiers. Mary threw a handful of dirt on top, then I did, too. Father shook Uncle James's hand, murmured a few words to Aunt Ida and left.

I stared down at the pine box, the frozen clumps of dirt on top. I felt lost. Utterly lost. Aunt Ida beside me; Uncle James, Patrick, Catherine, Mary and Duncan nearby—yet I was alone. *Things can change in a minute*, Mam had told me. I didn't know she meant an entire life.

There was only Mam in the grave, but the marker would say Mam, Da and Fred's names. Aunt Ida and Uncle James had wanted to put Bertie's name there, too, but I had argued so heatedly against it, they'd said they would wait a while. With so many markers to be carved, it would be a long time before this one was ready, anyway.

"It's cold. Let's go," Aunt Ida urged.

We walked through the cemetery, stopping briefly at the new graves where we'd buried Granny and Grandpa, and Aunt Helen the day before. Heads lowered against the wind, we picked our way among scores of yawning dark holes in the snow-covered ground. Black and white. That is what my world had become.

As we made our way back to Duncan's house, a commotion at the bakery across the street from us caught our attention. A police wagon and a car stood, doors open, as police officers and soldiers swarmed around the front of the shop.

"That's Martha Schultz's place," I told Aunt Ida.

Two men dragged a third between them out the door of the business. Martha and her mother followed and pulled at the uniformed men from behind. Martha's mother wailed.

"What's going on?" I asked.

"Wait here," Uncle James said. He crossed the street to speak to a soldier. After a moment he returned.

"They're arresting all the Germans in the city until they know the exact cause of the explosion," he explained.

"That's ridiculous," Aunt Ida said.

"People are upset. They don't feel safe," Uncle James explained. "The police thought they'd feel better if they put the Germans under lock and key for a while."

"It's what my father would have done," Catherine said unexpectedly. She straightened her doll's coat and smoothed its hair.

"Martha's family aren't spies," I said.

The door to the police wagon slammed shut, and the

men climbed into their various vehicles and left. Martha's mother threw her apron over her head and fled into the bakery. Martha stood staring down the now empty street.

"Go speak to your friend," Aunt Ida suggested.

Reluctantly, I crossed the street to Martha. I wasn't sure I wanted to talk to her. She had picked the other girls as friends over me at school, and had deserted me again after the explosion.

Face white with shock, she watched me come. "They took Papa, Rose," she said. "They arrested him." She began to cry.

Suddenly, it didn't matter to me what she'd done. It seemed so long ago.

"I'm sorry, Martha. They'll let him go soon. My aunt Ida says it wasn't a German invasion and people will soon realize that—"

"Martha! Martha! Come in. Don't stand in the street for the neighbours to see," her mother called from inside the bakery.

"Mama is terribly embarrassed," Martha said. "We were getting the bakery ready to open again, when they took Papa. Now I don't know what we will do." She looked across the street to where Aunt Ida and Uncle James waited for me. The others had gone ahead. "You buried your mama today. I heard you lost many of your family. I'm so sorry for your sadness," Martha said, her accent thick with distress. She took my hand. "We are both sad today."

I gave her a quick hug, and rejoined Aunt Ida and Uncle James.

"Rose, do you know Catherine's father's name?" Aunt Ida asked as we continued down the street.

I shook my head. "She's bragged about him often enough, but she never mentioned his name. I think he's a general in the army, from what she says."

Uncle James raised his eyebrows. "A general? Well, he shouldn't be hard to track down, then."

Mr. MacDonald greeted us at the door. "I have news for you. A friend of mine knows of a house to rent. Just half of it, mind you—but still, it's yours if you want it. You can move in right away."

"You make it sound like we want them to leave," Duncan's mother scolded. She flapped a dishrag at her husband.

He looked sheepish. "No. No," he protested. "James knows I don't mean it like that."

"We'll be delighted to have our own place," Uncle James assured them both. "You've been very kind taking care of Ida and the children, but we have to start again sometime and it might as well be now. I'll go to the relief office and see about some household supplies, furniture, and, of course . . ." He stopped.

Money, I thought. Only money made adults stop

speaking that abruptly. We would need money for rent and to buy food and clothes. Uncle James didn't have a job right now, and he had all our mouths to feed. I worried again that he and Aunt Ida might have to put us in an orphanage.

"Perhaps you should come too, Ida. You know what you need to set up a household more than I do," he suggested.

"I'll help you, Aunt Ida," Mary said.

"I'll get the wagon to help move things," Duncan offered. "If you don't need me for milk deliveries, that is, Dad," he added hastily.

His father shook his head. "Hopefully, next week we can get back to business as usual. People need milk even if their houses are falling down around their ears."

Aunt Ida pulled on her gloves. "Catherine. What is your father's name? We want to make inquiries. Let him know what's happened. He probably has already contacted the relief office looking for you. He must be worried sick. I should have thought of it before."

Catherine laid her doll on the table and began to strip off its coat. "Are you cold, Dolly?"

"Catherine?" Aunt Ida said.

We all stared, as Catherine calmly undressed her doll.

Aunt Ida placed her hands on Catherine's shoulders and swung her around. "What's your father's name?"

Catherine bit her lip. "I don't know."

"What do you mean you don't know?"

She squirmed, but Aunt Ida held her tight. "I never knew who my father was," she said in a rush. "It was just Mother and me for a while in Toronto. Then she got ill and died, and I came here to live with Grandmother."

"But you said he was a general in the army," I exclaimed. "What about all those presents he sent you from Paris?"

Catherine lowered her head. "I just made up those things," she mumbled. "Grandmother bought me the dresses."

"You lied!"

"I just wanted you all to like me at school," Catherine explained. She fiddled with the doll's dress. "You wouldn't like me if you knew I didn't have a father."

Wanted us to like her? She'd bossed everyone in the play yard. She'd made my life miserable, and it had all been a lie! I stalked outside. Patrick was shovelling a path to the stables for Mr. MacDonald. I went up to him.

"She lied," I said.

"Who lied?" Patrick asked.

"Catherine. Her father isn't a general in the army. She doesn't even know who he is," I stated flatly.

"Why she'd do that?" He leaned on his shovel.

"She says the girls at school wouldn't have liked her if they knew the truth."

"She's probably right." Patrick went on with his work.

I stared at him. "Patrick, do you have friends at school?"

"Sure."

"Name them."

"Well, Ernest—"

"He's your cousin. He has to be friends with you," I interrupted.

"No, he doesn't," Patrick argued.

"He's family, not a friend," I pointed out.

"It doesn't matter," he said. He banged the shovel on a piece of ice, breaking it. "I have lots of friends. You're just mad because you don't have any friends at all."

"I do, too," I protested.

"You're too homely and dumb to have friends."

"You take that back," I yelled. We couldn't seem to say two words to each other without arguing.

Aunt Ida and Uncle James came out with Catherine between them. She carried a small bag in one hand, the doll in the other. Her eyes were red-rimmed.

"Rose. Patrick. Please come here," Aunt Ida called. "We're going to take Catherine with us to the relief office. There will have to be a search for any living family members. They'll take care of her there," Aunt Ida said.

Put her in an orphanage is what she meant.

"But I want to stay with Rose," Catherine wailed.

"I am sorry, dear, but we don't have the money or space to take care of you. There's probably someone looking for you right now. You'll be well cared for."

Duncan pulled up with the wagon, Mary seated beside him.

I stared at Catherine for a long time. I'd take the old Catherine over this strange new one any day. She looked so lost. I put a hand on her arm. "I'll come visit you," I told her. "As soon as you're settled, let me know and I'll visit you."

Uncle James helped Catherine into the wagon.

"It's for the best," Aunt Ida assured me. "She doesn't seem too well. She'll get some help and then—Well, she's very pretty. I imagine some nice family will take her in."

She climbed up on the wagon seat beside Mary. "Please pack up our belongings as much as you can, Rose, while we're gone. Your uncle wants to move today."

I nodded.

As the wagon left the yard, I rounded on Patrick. "We can't ever fight again," I said.

"Why not?"

"Do you want to be sent away like Catherine? Aunt Ida and Uncle James might not be able to take care of all of us. And if they can't, we could end up in an orphanage." And with my limp red hair and freckles, there would be no nice family willing to take me in.

Patrick's eyes widened. "They wouldn't do that. We're family."

"There's you and me, Mary, and Ernest and Winnie when they come out of the hospital. And Bertie," I added defiantly. "That's a lot of people for Aunt Ida and Uncle James to take care of. And what if they want their own family someday? We might be in the way."

"But I don't want to go to an orphanage," Patrick said.

"So we have to be good and help out a lot. And don't eat so much. And no calling me dumb." I put that in for good measure.

"You can't call me fat," Patrick said.

Reluctantly, I nodded my agreement. I'd do anything to stay with Aunt Ida and Uncle James. Even be nice to Patrick. It also meant guarding my secret day and night. They would send me away for sure if they knew I'd caused the explosion.

Chapter 17

A bang and a muffled oath jerked me from sleep. I always woke the same way these days—with a jolt and a pounding heart. In the dim morning light of our bedroom, I saw Mary move about. We rented two rooms in the upper half of a house and shared the kitchen downstairs with the people in the bottom half. But as Aunt Ida repeated many times, it was a roof over our heads. She said that so many times, I knew she was trying to convince herself. A bride should have a nice home with her husband, I thought, not be stuck in two rooms with someone else's children. I only hoped she didn't see it that way.

Mary bumped into my bed again. "Drat it," she muttered.

"What are you doing?" I asked.

"Did I wake you? I'm sorry," she said. "But since you're awake . . ." She swept back the curtains. "Now I can at least see. I'm going to be black and blue from stumbling around this room. It's so different from our other bedroom. I guess I'll get used to it in time."

She might—but I'd never get used to this new bedroom, to half my family gone. I burrowed beneath the blankets and watched as Mary buttoned her skirt—a skirt that came from the relief office, like my bed, and the blankets, and the curtains on the windows. Mary bent to search beneath the bed.

"Why are you dressed up? Are you going back to the bank?" I asked. Mary had not been to work since the explosion.

"No," she said. "Ah! Here it is." She held up a shoe triumphantly, then sat on the bed to put it on. "I'm going to the relief office. I thought I'd volunteer my clerical skills. I'm sure they could use all the help they can get."

"What about the bank?"

"I can't go back there, Rose. I feel a fool. Such silly hopes for Horace. I'm afraid I became quite uppity with the other girls there. I couldn't face them." She gave a half laugh. "Not that it matters. I doubt I have a position there anymore. I said some pretty awful things to Horace the day of the explosion, and then I stormed out. I was just a good-time girl to him, Rose. No one special. Certainly no one he would marry. Mam knew that, but I was so headstrong." She stood. "So that's the end of my dreams," she said briskly.

"Mam didn't mind you having dreams," I told her. "She and Da were proud of you."

Mary sat back down and put her hand over mine. "Thank you, Rose. So, do you have any dreams?"

I thought about that one. I didn't think so. When

every minute of the day was filled with worry and terror of school, books, Sister Frances and the other girls, there wasn't much time left for dreams. Except that once I had thought I might be a teacher. I guess that was a dream, even though it didn't last long.

"Not really," I finally said.

"It's a hard time to dream," Mary said softly. "Anyway, I'm off to a new start." She stood and smoothed down her skirt. "I need to be busy and I need to help someone else. It takes a person out of themselves. I only wish I could bring in a bit of money for Aunt Ida and Uncle James. I'll keep a lookout for another paying position."

I wanted to ask her if she thought we'd be sent to an orphanage, then realized that Mary was too old for an orphanage. Maybe she could take care of us if Aunt Ida and Uncle James couldn't. I felt my hopes rise. But that wasn't fair. How could we tie down Mary, who yearned for so much?

"You should still dream," I told her.

"Well, you never know. I just might." She smiled and left.

I pushed back the covers and climbed out of bed. The room was cramped, even though it held only two narrow iron beds and a small table with a basin and pitcher. A cupboard with our clothes stood in the hallway outside, unable to fit in the room. The hall landing was also where Patrick slept on a cot. Aunt Ida and

Uncle James slept in the other room. I wasn't sure where we'd put Winnie and Ernest when they came home from the hospital.

I felt a twinge of guilt as I splashed water on my face. I still had not visited either of them. I had returned the nurse's cape to Camp Hill Hospital, but had run quickly in and right back out again without seeing anyone, and that included Sister Therese. I thought of her rosary pushed deep into the pocket of my coat. I'd never used it. I didn't say prayers anymore. They might be answered.

I locked eyes with myself in the mirror over the basin. I no longer looked like me—Rose. My face was thinner, cheekbones too pronounced, freckles redder than ever, hair straggly. Mam would hate me looking so dishevelled. I grabbed a comb and attacked the tangles, then gave up and threw the comb down. Even the clothes I wore weren't mine—neither stitched by Mam nor knitted by Granny. I had nothing left of me.

Downstairs in the kitchen, Aunt Ida hurriedly dried dishes. "Try to get down a little earlier, Rose," she said. "We only have so much time to use the stove."

We cooked and ate our meals first, then a family of seven used the kitchen.

"There's oatmeal in that pot." Aunt Ida nodded with her head to the stove. "And tea. But before you eat, could you please wake Patrick?"

I went to the bottom of the stairs and shouted up.

"Patrick! Aunt Ida says if you don't get up now, you won't have time to eat." She hadn't said that, but the threat of no breakfast would get Patrick up faster than any other.

"Where's Uncle James?" I asked as I helped myself to porridge.

"He went to help clear away some of the wreckage on the docks. No one can work until it's done," Aunt Ida said. "Though he has another of his headaches." She sounded worried.

The bump on Uncle James's head had left him with severe headaches. The doctor said they would go away eventually, but for now they plagued him daily.

A newspaper sat on the table. I ate a spoonful of porridge, then opened the paper to the only page that interested me: the one that carried advertisements put in by people searching for missing family members. More important, it had a list describing the unidentified injured and dead, updated every day. Laboriously, I sounded out the words. *Male. Age about 35. Black hair and moustache. Fleece-lined underwear. Blue cotton shirt.*

Patrick staggered through the room to the outhouse, then back in and flopped into a chair.

"Breakfast is on the stove," I said.

With a sigh he got to his feet and spooned porridge from the pot into a bowl. He still expected someone to serve him, Aunt Helen had spoiled him so. He poured milk over top and brought it back to the table. Abruptly he yanked the newspaper from my hands and spread it out next to his bowl.

"Hey, I was reading that," I protested.

"No, you weren't. You can't read." Patrick laughed, exposing a mouthful of grey porridge.

"Give it back," I cried.

"Children," Aunt Ida scolded. "Stop fighting and eat."

Fighting! I kicked Patrick hard beneath the table and widened my eyes at him. Only two days and we'd already forgotten our promise to each other to not fight. Patrick grimaced, so I knew he'd got my message, but he still didn't give me back the newspaper

"What do you want it for, anyway? You're not looking for anyone," I muttered.

"Well, who are you looking for?" Patrick asked.

"Bertie," I told him.

He shot a quick glance at me. "I'll look for you," he offered.

I wanted to do it myself. I was afraid he'd be careless and miss an advertisement. But I had to admit he could read faster, and Aunt Ida wanted us out of the kitchen.

"Nothing matches his description," Patrick said after a moment. "Nor my Dad's."

I looked up, surprised. I hadn't known Patrick still hoped his father was alive.

"That's it. We have to leave." Aunt Ida took the bowls from us.

"I'm not done," Patrick protested.

"Next time, come down earlier," Aunt Ida snapped. I'd never seen her so irritable.

"But . . ."

I kicked Patrick again, and he glared at me but said nothing further.

Aunt Ida quickly rinsed and put away the bowls. "Out," she said.

Patrick grabbed the newspaper from the table.

As we went upstairs, I turned to Aunt Ida. "Can we put an advertisement in the paper for Bertie?"

"Oh, Rose." She sighed. "I guess it couldn't hurt. I'll ask James to insert it. But please don't get your hopes up."

"Thank you." I hugged her tightly.

"Now, if you would tidy the beds, please, I'm going to the hospital to see Ernest. Are either of you coming with me?" Aunt Ida looked at me pointedly.

"We have plans," Patrick said quickly.

I glanced at him in surprise. I didn't know we had plans, but if it got me out of a hospital visit, I'd go along with him.

"Rose, you haven't been once to see Ernest or Winnie," Aunt Ida said. "Even Patrick's visited your brother."

"I'll go tomorrow," I promised recklessly. "But Patrick's right. We have plans." I didn't even feel bad about the lie. Lies didn't matter now that I didn't go to confession anymore. I quashed the thought that it would have mattered a great deal to Mam.

Aunt Ida raised her eyebrows. "Very well. Tomorrow. I have some items I need from the store. I'll give you children a list, if you'd please pick them up after your . . . plans. And be sure to comb your hair, Rose, before you go out. It looks dreadful."

She went into her bedroom. Patrick flopped down on his cot.

"Get off so I can make your bed," I ordered. "Though you really should make it yourself. I'm not your maid."

Patrick got to his feet, but ignored me, engrossed in the newspaper.

"What plans do we have?" I asked him.

He looked somewhat embarrassed. "It's something that I saw in here." He pointed to a page.

"What?"

"I wondered—" He stopped. "It says here that there is going to be a funeral for some of the unidentified bodies from the Chebucto Road School this morning. A 'mass funeral,' the newspaper calls it." He spoke in a rush. "I want to go, and I wondered if you'd go with me."

I stopped straightening the blankets.

"My Dad might be one of them," he continued. "I want to go just in case. I'm the only person left alive in my family to see him . . . to see him buried. I'll check the newspaper every day for Bertie if you'll come with me. I don't want to go alone."

I had been so wrapped up in my own misery, I hadn't even thought for one minute how Patrick must feel all on his own. At least I had Mary and Ernest and Winnie, and maybe Bertie.

"You don't have to check the newspaper for me," I said. "I'll go with you. Da or Fred might be there, too. Should we tell Aunt Ida?"

"No," Patrick said. "It would upset her."

I saw the sense of that and nodded. "Let me finish the beds."

The large number of wagons and relief vehicles had churned the roads to a thick, cloying mud. At first I tried to step around the ankle-deep puddles to save my boots, but soon gave that up and splashed through them.

"Should we have gone to Mass first?" Patrick asked.

I shrugged. "There will probably be lots of prayers and church stuff at the funeral," I said. I didn't want to go to Mass. I'd been only once since the explosion, and hated it. We'd gathered in a hall because the church was destroyed. The familiar words were spoken, and the incense, the altar boys and the priest were the same, but the peace they had once brought me was gone.

A large crowd had gathered outside the Chebucto

Road School yard beneath a sky heavy with low-slung clouds. Patrick and I wormed our way to the front and peered through the close-packed bodies to see coffins laid in rows. Two small boys climbed a nearby fence and shouted joyfully at the heights scaled, but found themselves rudely plucked from their perch and soundly scolded for their disrespect.

I stared in disbelief at the number of coffins that stretched as far as my eyes could see. The past eleven days, I'd heard the number of dead repeated: one thousand, some said; more like two thousand, others announced. My brain couldn't picture that many people. To see the numerous coffins laid out in front of me made it real. Was Da or Fred in one of them? Uncle Lyle? It didn't matter. So many coffins—I would surely know someone who lay within. A small bouquet of flowers lay on top of each one, and to see the bright blooms made my breath catch in a sob.

Churchmen huddled in a group, black hats pulled low against a biting wind. There was no way to know which church the dead attended, so all the ministers and priests were invited to speak. I could see Duncan standing to one side with a group of undertakers, the delivery wagon ready to bear coffins to the various cemeteries. He occasionally blew on his hands to warm them. Behind me, a woman cried quietly, and a man beside her wiped his eyes with a handkerchief.

A band played a hymn, then Father McManus

stepped forward and began a prayer. His voice sounded weak and thin in the open air, no wood beams and stone arches to catch his words and send them on to Heaven. One after another, the churchmen spoke, but I didn't hear them. Instead, I fought my own battle with God. I hadn't spoken to Him since the day after the explosion, but now I silently screamed at Him. *How could You let this happen to us? To me? Don't You care? Of all my prayers, why did You choose to answer this one?*

I looked down to see my hand inside Patrick's. I didn't know if he had reached for mine, or I for his. Tears trembled on his eyelashes, though he blinked rapidly to hold them back. He looked so lonely and bewildered, I left my hand where it was.

The skies began to weep a cold rain that turned to ice when it hit the ground. Umbrellas mushroomed, and the churchmen scurried to the protection of their motor cars for the journey to the cemeteries.

My hand was abruptly released. I tucked it inside a pocket to keep warm.

As I turned away from the sight of the coffins being loaded in the various vehicles, I saw the red hair of a child carried in a woman's arms. She hurried toward the street.

"Bertie!" I shouted.

I thought I saw the child's head turn, but the woman was swallowed up by the crowd and I lost sight of them.

"That's Bertie," I said to Patrick. "Hurry."

We dodged about people as I frantically searched for the woman. Then, up ahead, I saw her again. If only she was close enough for me to see the child clearly. I began to run, but the crowd closed in and I lost her yet again.

"I think she's going to the railroad station," Patrick gasped. He puffed beside me, out of breath.

Suddenly, I slipped on the icy road and fell heavily. Air whooshed out of my lungs and my sore arm stung fiercely. Stunned, I lay there until hands helped me up.

"That's quite a fall, young lady," a man said.

"You've cut your knee, dear," a woman said. She dabbed at it with a handkerchief.

"No," I screamed. "Leave me alone." I pushed at the hands that held me, that kept me from Bertie.

The man and woman drew back, startled, and I ran off, Patrick close behind. We arrived at the station to see a train pull out in billows of white steam. I tore up and down the platform to see inside the windows of the passenger cars as they swept by. Finally at one, a white face topped by red hair peered back at me.

"There! There!" I pulled on Patrick's arm. "It's him. It's Bertie! Where is it going? Where is this train going? Read the schedule!" I yelled at him. I pushed him toward the station entrance where a board listed the arrivals and departures. I needed him to read it. I might get the station wrong.

"Just a minute." Patrick studied the printed schedule hung on the wall. "Truro. It's gone to Truro."

"We have to go there."

"We don't have a ticket or any money to buy one," Patrick pointed out. He examined the schedule again. "Besides, that was the last train today. The next one to Truro is tomorrow morning at ten o'clock."

"Then we'll go tomorrow and find Bertie."

Chapter 18

"This is dumb," Patrick announced. He stared morosely around the crowded train.

"Then why did you bother to come?" I asked. "I could have gone myself. I don't need you to help find Bertie." I was, in fact, relieved to have Patrick beside me on the hard train seat, but I wasn't about to tell him that.

I wiped steam fog from the train window with the back of a mitten and peered out at the snow-stippled fields that rushed past. I'd never been away from Halifax before and my stomach felt hollow with fear. I was determined, though. I had to find Bertie, and if I'd thought he was in Africa, well, I would have searched for him there.

"Nothing better to do," Patrick mumbled around a jawbreaker. He fished in the bag for a second one and popped it into his mouth.

He was right. There was nothing better to do. There was no school; there were no sleds to race down snow-packed hills and few friends to race against. Seeing those that remained only reminded us of who was gone, so we didn't go out much.

I leaned back against the seat and closed my eyes. The train car was overheated. It stank, too—an old smell of coal fumes from the endlessly burning stove at the end of the car, wet winter woollens, stale sandwiches and unwashed bodies.

"But it's still dumb," he said again. His lips were stained black from the candy and his cheeks bulged.

Patrick would never change. I wanted to snatch away the bag that he clutched tightly in his hand.

I'd bribed Patrick to secrecy with an offer to buy him candy with the lunch coins Aunt Ida had given me. I could have just told her why we were going to Truro, but I was afraid she'd stop me, so I said I was going to see Winnie. She'd been delighted. "I knew she'd come around given time," she'd told Uncle James happily.

I'd cringed when I heard that. Not telling the whole truth felt as bad as a complete lie, confession or no confession. I would go see Winnie, as I had said. Hopefully, that would make it less a fib—though the thought of visiting Winnie made my stomach quiver. If it wasn't for me, she wouldn't be in the hospital.

After a long while, the train lurched, shuddered and stopped. "Are we in Truro?" I asked Patrick.

He leaned over me to glance out the window. "That's what the sign says. Can't you read it?" he said. He grinned widely, pleased with his own joke.

We filed off the train with the other passengers, then stood on the platform while people milled about us.

"Now what?" Patrick asked.

I looked around uncertainly. I think I'd had it in my mind that if I got to Truro, Bertie would be at the station waiting for me. "Why don't we ask the ticket agent first?" I suggested. "We know the woman came to Truro."

"There were other places she could have got off," Patrick said.

"What do you mean?" I asked sharply.

"The train goes on to other towns. This isn't the only stop."

"Why didn't you tell me that before?" I yelled at him.

"I just thought of it now," he said. Behind us, the train chugged out, destined for those *other places*. Bertie could be anywhere.

"Well, we can start here." I pushed open the heavy station door and crossed the room to where a man sat on a stool behind a high wooden counter.

"Where to?" he asked.

"Nowhere," I replied.

He frowned at me over gold-coloured wire-framed glasses.

"I mean," I explained, hurriedly. "I wondered if you know a woman who took the train yesterday to Halifax. She had a red-haired boy with her, about four years old."

"Lots of women took the train yesterday and lots of four-year-old boys," the man replied. "Now, move along. You're holding up the line."

I glanced behind me, but only saw Patrick. "No. You don't understand. I think that boy is my brother. I'm from Halifax and he was lost in the explosion. I thought I saw him yesterday with a woman who got on the afternoon train for Truro."

The man's frown faded. He thought for a moment, then shook his head. "I can't remember. I see so many people."

"Thank you," I told him.

"Good luck with your search. Terrible thing that happened there. Terrible."

I went over to where Patrick was examining a large poster of a train going through mountains.

"Wouldn't it be great to take the train all the way out west? Right through the Rocky Mountains," he enthused.

"How can you think about that when Bertie is lost?" I demanded.

"I was just looking," he said.

"Well, start *looking* for Bertie," I said.

"Where?"

I mulled over the problem. "We'll ask at the shops. Everyone goes to the shops."

We left the station and walked toward downtown.

"It's not that big a place," Patrick said. "We should be able to find him if he's here." He stopped in front of a store window decorated with silver garland and holly. "They're having Christmas," he said. "Look at that coaster." He leaned closer to the window. "I bet it could go down the hill faster than anyone else's. I'll ask Mama for that for Christmas."

Startled, I stared at him. As I did, I saw his mouth turn down and his lips tremble as he became aware of what he'd said.

"I forgot is all," he muttered. "It felt so normal here that I forgot." He wiped a hand across his eyes and walked away.

I knew what he meant. At home the store windows were boarded up. Lamps and electric lights tried unsuccessfully to push back the resulting gloom. A few shops had sweets for the holidays and some carried toys, but the need for food and household goods was greater, and no one had money left over for anything else. Christmas might be in three days, but not for Richmond.

For hours, we wandered in and out of shops, Patrick on one side of the street, me on the other. No one knew where we could find Bertie.

"Trouble is, dearie," the clerk at the last store I went into said, "we've had so many strangers in town since the explosion, it's hard to keep track of anyone. People here to visit family in our hospital, children brought to stay with kin." She placed a bag of flour in a box for a woman customer. "Even some of those American doctors and nurses are here."

I thanked her and went outside to wait for Patrick. It

was hopeless. I'd never find Bertie. Perhaps, like every-one else believed, he was with Mam in Heaven.

Patrick wandered out of a flower shop, quite pleased with himself. "Look," he said. He held up two lollipops. "She gave me some candy."

"Candy!" I shouted. My temper flared. "Did you even ask about Bertie?" I didn't give him time to answer. "Candy and your stomach are all you ever give any mind to. You don't even care that your mother and father are dead!"

Patrick's face drained of colour. Abruptly, he drew back his arm and threw the lollipops as far away as he could. I felt stunned. I couldn't believe I'd said such hurtful words. Words that I knew weren't true.

Suddenly, the woman customer came flying out of the store. "Oh, I'm so glad I caught you, girl. I just remembered that Mrs. Halliday down on Prince Street took in some youngsters from Halifax. I remember see-ing her with a little fellow with red hair. You just go down Prince Street until you get to Pleasant—that's five blocks down. It's the blue house on the corner."

"Thank you."

"I hope it's your brother." She smiled and went back into the store.

Patrick stalked away from me.

"Wait." I ran to catch up to him. "Patrick, I'm sorry. I didn't mean it. I just . . ." How to explain that I wanted to hurt him because I was hurting. It made no sense.

"At night I close my eyes and pretend I'm home," he said. "Then I hear Aunt Ida or you or Mary, and I'm laying on a cot in the hall. I pretend I'm only visiting and I'll be home soon, but that doesn't work, either, because I know I won't ever go back there again."

I felt thoroughly ashamed. "I am so sorry. I shouldn't have said such awful things to you. I don't know why I did."

Patrick grimaced. "Aunt Ida yelled at me this morning. I never heard her yell before. Nobody's acting normal. Do you think they ever will?"

"I don't know."

We walked in silence for a few minutes. "Where are we going?" I asked.

"This is Prince Street," Patrick said. "I saw a sign back there. The woman said five blocks. We've come four, so the house must be just up here."

"Oh," I said quietly. "Thanks."

Patrick nodded, then pointed at a large, blue clapboard house that sat on the corner. "You think that's it? That big house?"

"I guess so."

My heart pounded as I knocked on the front door. I studied the garden, the brown weathered stocks that come summer would be covered with pink hollyhock blooms. I hadn't realized until then how relieved my eyes were to see whole houses and buildings, and gardens.

I heard footsteps, then the door swung open.

"Yes?" a woman said.

"Mrs. Halliday?"

"Yes."

"My name is Rose Dunlea, and I was told you had some children from the Halifax explosion staying here."

"Yes, I do. Come in."

Patrick snatched his cap from his head as we entered a large foyer. He gawked so much that I wanted to thump him for his ill manners.

"My little brother, Bertie—Albert Dunlea—is missing. He has red hair. A woman in a shop told me you had a boy here with red hair."

"I do, but his name isn't Albert. It's Gordon."

"Gordon? Are you sure?"

"That's what he said his name was. Would you like to see him?"

"Yes, please."

She led the way down a long hall. Patrick almost climbed up the back of my heels, he followed me so closely. I turned and glared at him.

"Sorry," he muttered.

The hall opened into a sun-washed kitchen. The woman went to a screened door. Patrick and I crowded in beside her to see five children in the yard.

"He's over there. At the bottom of the garden." Mrs. Halliday pointed to a small boy near the back fence. She opened the door. "Gordon," she called.

The boy turned around, but even before I saw his face I knew it wasn't Bertie. This boy was too stocky.

"That's not him," I said. I fought tears that threatened to spill over. I had wanted it so badly to be Bertie.

"I'm very sorry." The woman put a hand on my arm and pushed me into a chair. "Sit down. You children look all done in. Let me get you both a glass of milk and a sandwich."

"We don't want to be any trouble," I said, but I sank into the chair. My legs couldn't carry me any farther.

"Did you come from Halifax to look for your brother?" The woman bent and took a pitcher of milk and a slab of ham from an icebox. She had a calm, kind way about her that I immediately took to.

"We arrived on the train this morning," Patrick said. "Rose thought she saw her brother yesterday in Halifax, and then getting on the Truro train with a woman. We told our aunt Ida that we were coming to visit Winnie, Rose's sister. She's at the hospital here."

"I see." Mrs. Halliday cut bread and placed thick slices of ham inside. She put the sandwiches on a plate and set them and glasses of milk on the table before me and Patrick. Patrick tucked right into his. I took a bite, chewed, but found I couldn't swallow past the lump in my throat. I reached for the glass of milk. Mrs. Halliday sat down opposite us and picked up a sock she was darning. The needle flashed silver in and out of the wool, and I swear it could have been Mam sitting there.

"I wish Gordon was your brother," she said. "No one's come to claim him or two of the others. We've placed an advertisement in the Halifax paper to run tomorrow. Hopefully someone will see it and recognize the children. Some arrived here so little that they can't tell where they came from or who their parents are. I'm afraid they'll be separated forever." She glanced up from her needle. "If you two youngsters are here looking for your brother, your parents must be hurt . . ." *Or worse*, her eyes finished: sympathetic green eyes, not as brilliant as Mam's but with similar laugh lines spreading outward from the corners.

I took a second gulp of milk, hoping to wash down the stubborn lump of sandwich, but choked instead. Patrick thumped me hard on the back, nearly knocking me off the chair.

"Stop it," I gasped. Tears spilled over my cheeks. I tried desperately to stop them, but that made them fall harder.

The woman set down her sewing, came around the table and put an arm around my shoulders. "Hush, hush, dear."

"You don't understand," I cried. "I need to find Bertie. I have to."

Mrs. Halliday's arm tightened around me. I turned

and clung to her, and the story spilled out of me. I
couldn't stop the flood of words. Mam buried in the
cemetery. Da and Frederick dead. Winnie and Ernest
hurt. Bertie lost. Sister Frances. School. The way I'd
not talked to Da the morning of the explosion because I
was mad at him. The fact that I was slow.

"So I prayed to God and asked Him to make it so I
didn't have to go to school and He answered with the
explosion. I caused the explosion," I sobbed. "So I
thought if I could find Bertie, it might make it a bit
better."

Mrs. Halliday patted my back and handed me a
handkerchief. I mopped my eyes.

Patrick's chair screeched as he pushed it back from
the table. His mouth gaped open. "You caused the
explosion! I thought *I'd* caused the explosion!"

Chapter 19

"Oh, my. Such a burden you two have been carrying around." Mrs. Halliday returned to her seat across from us. She folded her hands on the table, sewing set aside.

My cheeks burned with embarrassment. "I'm so sorry. I didn't mean to cry . . . and you made us this nice lunch. You must think we're dreadful—"

Mrs. Halliday put her hand up to stop me. "Sometimes it's easier to talk to a stranger," she said.

She was right. I had told her things that I couldn't tell Aunt Ida. It might be that she reminded me so much of Mam.

"So I understand why Rose thinks she caused the explosion, but why do you think you did, Patrick?" Mrs. Halliday asked.

He ducked his head and twirled the milk glass around and around in his hand. "Well, I thought maybe God was punishing me." He shot a glance my way. "I tease people sometimes."

"Hah!" I exclaimed.

"I guess I'm not always nice," he mumbled.

He shifted nervously on his chair. "I tease Rose because she's dumb. She can't read properly or learn stuff."

"Rose doesn't strike me as the least bit dumb," Mrs. Halliday said. "She found her way to me in her search for her brother, and that takes some initiative and courage."

I wasn't sure what *initiative* was, but it sounded good. I did know about courage, though. Great-grandmother Rose had courage. Courage had brought her to Canada from Ireland. Had it brought me here to Truro? I felt better thinking I had courage like Great-grandmother Rose.

"I thought maybe God was teaching me a lesson," Patrick said.

"I'm not sure what church you go to, and I don't think it important that I do know," Mrs. Halliday said slowly. "I just want to say this: the God I know would never hurt people. Would yours, Rose? Patrick? Bad things happen. Occasionally, people intentionally cause them—like this war we're in—sometimes they're an accident, and sometimes they're the way of the natural world."

I sat for a long time, silent. I'd never thought it through before. Things had changed so fast, I hadn't had time. I just knew I had prayed to God to make it so I didn't have to go to school, and then the explosion happened.

A small girl came in from the backyard, and Mrs. Halliday put an arm around her and pulled her close, then after a quick word sent her back out to play. I

worried that I wasn't answering Mrs. Halliday fast
enough, but she didn't press me. She let me take my
time. I liked that. When Sister Frances tapped her foot
impatiently, my brain stopped dead. When I grew up,
I vowed, I would always give people time to think. I
focussed my thoughts on what Mrs. Halliday had said.

Was that it? Had the explosion been an accident? I
thought about St. Joseph's Church on a Sunday morning, and the peace that filled me as I bent my knee and
bowed my head in prayer. The saints who watched over
me. My talks with God.

"Maybe it was an accident," I said finally.

Mrs. Halliday nodded encouragingly.

"The two ships collided. Uncle James said one of the
pilots on board must have made a mistake. The one
ship had explosives and they blew up and that caused
the explosion. God wouldn't hurt that many people just
because I prayed for myself, would He?"

"Rose, people pray for themselves all the time. We're
selfish, but He understands that," Mrs. Halliday said.
"And Patrick . . ."

He grinned sheepishly.

"God wouldn't give you so hard a lesson. But I think
you've learned from the explosion, anyway."

"So, I didn't cause it?" Patrick asked.

"No," I told him. "And neither did I."

And I believed myself. I really did believe that my
prayer hadn't caused the explosion. I could have floated

right around Mrs. Halliday's kitchen, I felt so light right then.

"Now, you said you were going to see your sister, Winnie," Mrs. Halliday reminded me.

"Yes," I said. "She's at the hospital. Aunt Ida gave me a map of how to get there from the train station."

"Well, I suggest you go visit your sister. No more searching for Bertie today. When you get back to Halifax, tell your aunt Ida that you thought you saw him get on the train. She can contact the proper people, like the relief office and the police, and they can start a search for him. You should have told your aunt where you were going. Don't go off on your own again," she chided gently.

"We won't," I assured her.

Patrick wolfed down the rest of his sandwich and looked hungrily at mine.

"You can have it. I'm really not too hungry," I said, glancing apologetically at Mrs. Halliday.

After Patrick had eaten my lunch, too, we gathered ourselves up. Mrs. Halliday placed my hat firmly on my head.

"You look after yourself, Rose. And if you find Bertie, will you let me know?"

"I will," I promised. Suddenly my arms went around her neck and held on tight. "Thank you," I whispered.

"You're very welcome."

Patrick and I left the house and walked back the way we'd come.

"So you thought you'd caused the explosion?" he said.

"And you thought you had."

"But we didn't."

"No, we didn't," I said.

Patrick began to whistle and pulled out his bag of candy. I studied the map that Aunt Ida had drawn for us. We'd turned ourselves around by our trip to Mrs. Halliday's, but I could tell where we were.

"Here, let me see that," Patrick demanded.

I stuffed it into my pocket.

"Well, I hope you know where we're going," he said. He held out the paper bag. "Do you want a candy?"

I put my hand out, only to have the bag pulled away from my fingertips. He laughed and held it out again, this time letting me take a candy.

I hurried my steps, anxious now to get to Winnie. It had been nearly two weeks since I'd seen her last. I remembered the soldiers carrying her into the hospital. I missed her dreadfully. I'd make it up to her by telling her the best story I could.

As we walked, I formed my first prayer in a long time. *Please, God, help me find Bertie. Not just for myself,* I hastily added, *but for my family. And I'm sorry I didn't believe in You.* It felt good to talk to Him again.

At the hospital, I asked a nurse where Winnie could be found. She directed us upstairs to a long room with beds filled with children. More children sat at three small tables set in the middle of the room. They drew pictures or turned the pages of books. Winnie sat in a bed, propped up by two pillows.

"Rose," she yelled when she caught sight of us. She bounced on the bed.

I'd never been so glad to see anyone in my whole life. I hugged her gingerly, fearful of hurting her, though obviously nothing hurt too much, for she flung herself at me.

"You should have come before," she said accusingly.

"I know. I'm sorry. I'll explain why I didn't when we have lots of time," I told her.

Winnie smiled. "See what I got?" She held up a china doll. It reminded me suddenly of Catherine. I briefly wondered where she was right now.

"You can hold it," Winnie offered.

I'd forgotten how quickly Winnie forgave and forgot. I took the doll and admired it.

"And now you hold it, Patrick," she ordered.

He sighed, but picked the doll up by an arm, dangled it, then dropped it on the bed.

"And I got a huge cut on my stomach," Winnie said. She pulled up her nightgown to show me a large bandage. "It's sewed together. Do you want to see?" Her fingers reached toward the dressing.

"No. That's fine," I said hastily as I pulled down her nightgown.

"I also got a new storybook. When you're sick, everyone's extra nice to you," she confided. She plopped the book in my lap. "Do you want to read it?"

I opened it, but as usual the letters jumped around and I couldn't make sense of any of the words. "It looks very nice," I said weakly, and closed the book.

A nurse came and stuck a thermometer in Winnie's mouth.

"It's good, but not as good as your stories," Winnie declared around the thermometer.

"Keep your mouth closed," the nurse ordered.

Winnie grimaced, but did as told.

"She's making excellent progress," the nurse said to me. "I understand your aunt and uncle are Winnie's guardians now that her parents are dead?"

I saw a shadow darken Winnie's eyes. I had wondered if she knew Mam and Da were gone. She did.

At first I didn't really know what the nurse meant by "guardian," then realized it was what Catherine's grandmother was for her, so I nodded. I guessed that meant Aunt Ida and Uncle James were also my guardians and Ernest's and Patrick's. If we had guardians, surely we wouldn't go to an orphanage.

"Well, please tell them that we are sending Winnie back to Halifax to Victoria General Hospital at week's end. Now that things have settled down there, they have room to take her for her convalescence. She'll be closer to her family."

The nurse took the thermometer from Winnie's mouth.

"Rose tells the best stories. She's going to tell me one now," Winnie said to the nurse as soon as her mouth was free.

"Are you?"

The nurse looked around the room, which was full of children. "Do you mind if some of the other children listen? It's a long day for them, stuck in here. Many don't have any family to visit."

I stared at her, aghast. She wanted me to tell a story to the whole room? I could feel my legs begin to tremble. It was just like being asked to read at school. Taking my silence as agreement, the nurse gathered the children around Winnie's bed. Some sat and some lay on the floor. Others crawled to the ends of their beds to hear.

I swallowed hard. "What do you want to hear?" I asked Winnie.

"A story about Great-grandmother Rose," Winnie replied.

I thought with a pang of the Irish Chain quilt. I didn't know if I could tell a story of Great-grandmother without the quilt. "Are you sure?" I asked. "What about the princess in the Citadel? Maybe the children would rather hear about her."

"No, one about Great-grandmother Rose," Winnie repeated firmly.

I closed my eyes and imagined Winnie and me back in our room on Albert Street, just the two of us. I remembered then a small patch from the quilt, a faded grey wimsey cut from a work dress. I took a deep breath.

"After forty-five days on a ship crossing the ocean from Ireland, Great-grandmother Rose and her three children arrived at Quebec. So many were sick on board that they quarantined the passengers. For three weeks, Rose lived in a corner of a shed, the family sleeping on a bed of straw. When it came time to leave the island in the middle of the vast St. Lawrence River, Rose asked, 'Where do I go?'

"She was in a strange land that she knew nothing about. A kindly man told her to take a steamer to Toronto, where work was plentiful for new immigrants. With the last of the priest's money, Rose bought passage for herself and her children on a steamer ship and went to Toronto. Canada was a big country, and Rose felt frightened by the thick stands of trees that crowded down to the riverbanks. When she arrived in Toronto, Rose left the ship and stood on the dock, lonely and scared. She had no money and nobody to turn to." I paused a moment to let the words sink into the children. I knew it was the same for them. Since the explosion, we all felt like strangers in a bewildering new land.

"Rose went into the Widows' and Orphans' Home. The rules were strict and difficult to live by, but it was a roof over their heads and food in their stomachs. Then one day the head of the home came to her. 'Your son is ten years old and we have arranged for him to work on a farm.' And she took him away. A few days later the head came to Rose again. 'Your older daughter is eight and we have arranged for her to train as a domestic in a doctor's house.' And she took her away. Now Rose had only one child left with her, my grandma. At first she could think of nothing but the empty spot in her heart, but then she vowed she would bring her family back together."

Suddenly I was hearing the words of my story as if for the very first time. They rang in my heart, and I knew I'd found the key to the quilt. It had been inside me all along, just needing to be brought out.

I had courage like Great-grandmother Rose.

"Rose went out and got work as a cook at a boarding house. She worked hard for two years, and earned enough money to buy passage for her family to Halifax. 'I want to be as near Ireland as I can,' she said. She went to the farm and got her son, and went to the doctor's house and got her daughter, and they were all together again."

At the end of the story, there was a moment of silence, then everyone clapped. Embarrassed, I realized the nurses and a couple of doctors had also stopped to listen. My cheeks turned crimson at the attention.

"Stories are for bedtime," a voice announced loudly.

My head whipped around. On the floor, dressed in a cap and coat, was a red-haired boy.

"Bertie!"

Chapter 20

I sat on my bed, working out a new story to tell the children at Victoria General Hospital. I went in regularly now, twice a week, to tell them a story, then stayed to help them with their afternoon snack. It had all come about from my visits with Winnie there. The nurses said I had a wonderful way with children, and Sister Therese said I had a wonderful way with words.

She told me that a kindergarten would soon be set up for the little ones, to get them off the streets until school could be started up again. Then she asked me to help out at the kindergarten. I hadn't told Aunt Ida yet, but Sister Therese had said there would be a small stipend for me. I kept that part secret because I wanted to surprise Aunt Ida when I handed her my first wages.

Today, though, my mind wandered away from my story planning. Six weeks after the explosion, our lives had fallen into a pattern of sorts. Slowly, we were becoming used to each other in this new household, though some people, like Patrick, took more getting used to than others. I could hear him, Bertie and Ernest laughing all the way upstairs from the kitchen. Aunt Ida said she had no idea boys could be so noisy. I will say this for Patrick, though, he certainly did bring Ernest out of himself. I'd worried dreadfully when Ernest first came home, black patch over one eye and so silent. Patrick had immediately dragged him outside to show him a new sled Uncle James had got for them.

Bertie suddenly ran in and jumped on the bed beside me.

"Stop that, you little monkey." I pulled him down into my arms. "You'll break the bed. It's not that strong."

I tickled him until he squealed, then hugged him.

I still couldn't get over the miracle of Bertie. He was our family's Christmas gift. Blown out of the house by the force of the explosion, he'd been picked up by a soldier, who had taken him to hospital. He was uninjured, but the shock of it all had locked his tongue. He'd been sent to Truro and taken in by a kindly woman, Mrs. Elliott. He hadn't said a single word until the day he saw me at the Truro hospital with Winnie. I don't know who was more shocked—me or Mrs. Elliott. She'd taken Bertie to the hospital to distribute Christmas toys to the children, and they'd stopped to listen to my story. She had a large heart, Mrs. Elliott did, but as she appeared so attached to Bertie, I often wondered if she regretted going to the hospital that particular day. Aunt Ida had promised her we would always keep in touch.

Bertie struggled to be free of my arms. "I'm going sledding with Ernest and Patrick," he announced.

"Go, then." I pushed him off the bed. Already he thought himself too old for hugs.

As our household settled down, I had more time to think, mostly about the explosion. I still have trouble believing it really happened. A stubborn part of my mind still clings to the thought that it was all a nightmare, but the shattered trees, destroyed buildings and, mostly, the graves in the cemetery rudely remind me every day that it was not.

I still don't know why bad things happen. I go over it time and time again. I know we all have good and bad in our lives, though some folks seem to have more than their fair share of one over the other. Granny Dunlea would say hard times make us stronger, Aunt Helen would say they're meant to test our mettle and Mam would say it's God's will. I don't know what I say. I wonder if I ever will.

Mary appeared in the doorway of the bedroom. "Rose, Uncle James said they are going to start to clear the rubble away from the house. I want to go back before they do and see if there's anything left. Anything at all . . ." She paused. "Do you want to come with me?"

Suddenly, I wanted to go back, badly. I had not been to Albert Street since the day of the explosion. I grabbed my coat and followed her outdoors.

In the cold light of a late January morning, we stood looking down at Richmond. A desolate landscape of grey, brown and white stretched before us, not a trace of colour anywhere to relieve our eyes. Snow rippled across the ground, pushed by the wind into life, but its promise was false; nothing lived here anymore. For a moment I saw it whole again: houses and stores standing, schools with children in the yards, streets full of delivery wagons, women shaking rugs on front porches and gossiping to each other.

"It breaks my heart," Mary said brokenly.

With her words, my fantasy burst and the flattened city spread out before me once more.

"Let's get on with it, then," Mary said. "Duncan said he'll meet us with the wagon in case we find anything usable. I don't want to keep him waiting."

We passed Schultz's bakery, and Martha came to the door and waved us over. Warm, yeast-scented air enveloped us as we went in.

"Have a bun." Mr. Schultz handed a soft roll to each of us. As Mary thanked him, I stepped away with Martha.

"You have a new house," Martha said.

I nodded. "Aunt Ida and Uncle James are our guardians now." I'd finally asked Aunt Ida if we would be going to an orphanage, and she'd swept me up in a huge hug and said, "Never."

"I see the police let your father go."

"He was only away a week. But it's just now that people are beginning to come for our baking again,"

Martha said. "It takes time for them to forget, if ever."

I broke open the bun and released a fragrant aroma that made my mouth water. Martha moved behind the counter and stacked loaves of bread.

"I won't be going back to school," she said. "I'm working here now. Mama and Papa need me."

"I'm to work at the new kindergarten," I told her shyly. "And Sister Therese said she'd help me with my reading."

"Rose," Mary called, "we must go."

"Come by and visit me," Martha said, as we left.

"I will."

We picked our way around piles of debris to Albert Street and our house. We were stopped twice by soldiers, but Mary showed them the pass she had, and they waved us on our way.

Then we were there. At our house. I began to tremble. Why had I thought I could do this? See our life in bits and pieces. My teeth chattered so hard I feared I'd break them.

"I expect most everything was lost in the fire, but I need to be sure," Mary said. She didn't notice me frozen to the spot. She threw a board aside and bent down to sift through the rubble.

"Oh, look, Rose," Mary exclaimed happily. She held up a cup and saucer. "It's one of Mam's best. And it's not even chipped! Imagine that."

She set it carefully down. That teacup broke the spell

that rooted my feet. We dug for an hour, finding small treasures—like Da's cap. A hole was burned through the peak, but we set it with the teacup and saucer.

As I tossed boards aside, I saw a scrap of material sticking out from a pile of plaster. A dress, I thought as I tugged hard. It suddenly came free, throwing ash and dust into my face. I coughed, then turned the material over in my hand. Burned, it crumbled beneath my fingers, but not before I recognized what it was. I sadly brushed soot from the only small piece I could salvage: Great-grandmother Rose's wedding dress patch. All that was left of the Irish Chain quilt. Sadly, I thrust it into my pocket.

"Help me with this, Rose," Mary called.

I ran over to find her struggling with the chest from our bedroom.

"The top's burned," she gasped as she yanked it from beneath a pile of boards. "But I bet Uncle James could make a new one for it."

We dragged it to the front lawn. I brushed off soot, then pried open the lid. Mary pulled out a couple of sweaters.

"They stink to high Heaven of damp and smoke," she said.

She added them to the growing pile of items we would keep.

I plunged my hand to the bottom of the chest and searched. My fingers touched a bag. The patches I'd collected for my own quilt. I grabbed a handful and spread them across my skirt. They, too, reeked of smoke, but as they were mostly cotton, I knew a good wash would take care of that.

I stroked the remnants of Mam's housedress, Granny's apron, Aunt Helen's blouse—I would give that to Patrick if he wanted it—Bertie's nightgown, and for the first time in six weeks felt a small glow of happiness. My family had been given back to me.

I stuffed the material back into the bag. I would make them into my own Irish Chain quilt, and one day—not right now, and probably not for a while—I would point to a patch and tell the story of Mam threatening to give us a good hiding, Fred's forgetfulness, Grandpa's false teeth, Granny and Aunt Helen and The Illnesses, or Da singing "My Wild Irish Rose."

My wild Irish Rose,
the sweetest flower that grows.
You may search everywhere
but none can compare
with my wild Irish Rose.

Author's Note

In 1917, a child with dyslexia was considered "slow" or "simple." Today we know that dyslexia is a learning disability. People with dyslexia are as intelligent as other people. It is not a disease, but a difference in the brain; dyslexics have minds that learn differently. A person with dyslexia has problems making sense of what is seen or heard. While children today can receive help from teachers and parents, special schools and tutors, some of the stigma of having dyslexia remains. Dyslexics struggle with poor self-image, social difficulties, fear of failure, frustration and anger—the same problems my character Rose faces in *Irish Chain*.

On December 6, 1917, Halifax experienced Canada's greatest human tragedy. Two ships, one loaded with explosives, collided in the Narrows, resulting in the largest man-made explosion outside of Hiroshima. Estimates put the dead between two and three thousand. The working-class north end of Halifax, Richmond, was completely devastated. But, as all people who survive tragedy and loss throughout the ages have done, the people of Halifax, with the generous support of Canadians and Americans, rebuilt their lives, demonstrating once again the enduring spirit of humankind.

All the characters in *Irish Chain* are products of my imagination, with the exception of two. Sister Maria Cecilia was the principal of St. Joseph's School and Father McManus was one of the priests at St. Joseph's Church at the time of the explosion. I have used their names, but otherwise, their characters in the book are fictionalized.

The lyrics and music to "My Wild Irish Rose" were written by Chauncey Olcott for his production of *A Romance of Athlone*. The music was published in 1899.

Visit my Web site for a teacher/student resource page on the Halifax Explosion.

http://www.barbarahaworthattard.com

Wreckage at Richmond.   *From the collection of the Maritime Museum of the Atlantic, Halifax, Nova Scotia, Canada*

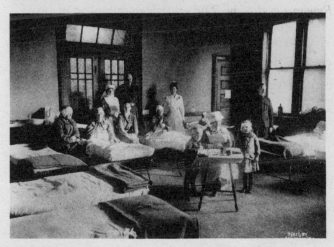

YMCA Emergency hospital.   *From the Kitz collection, Maritime Museum of the Atlantic, Halifax, Nova Scotia, Canada*

Ruins of St. Joseph's School and St. Joseph's Church.
From the collection of the Maritime Museum of the Atlantic, Halifax,
Nova Scotia, Canada

Acknowledgements

Many thanks to Marge Eaton, Heather Haworth, Mary McGinn, Roberta Guildford and Judy Ann Sadler for their help with various aspects of this book.

Thank you to the Ontario Arts Council for a grant provided to the author.

Nine Patch Quilt Pattern

A single Irish Chain quilt uses a block pattern called "Nine Patch." Nine Patch blocks were the first blocks children leaned to make when they were old enough to sew. The instructions below call for blue and white fabric, but you can choose any two colours, as long as one is dark and one is light.

You'll need
- a pencil
- a rulcr
- cereal-box cardboard
- scissors
- .25 m (¼ yd.) blue cotton fabric (plain or print)
- .25 m (¼ yd.) white cotton fabric (plain or print)
- straight pins
- a sewing needle and thread
- an iron (ask an adult to help)

Instructions
1 Draw a 13-cm (5-in.) square on the cereal-box cardboard and cut it out. This will be your pattern, or template, as it is called in quilting.

2 Place the template on the blue fabric and trace around it with the pencil. Cut out the fabric square exactly on the lines. Use this same method to cut out four more blue squares.

3 Use the above method to cut out four white squares. You should now have five blue squares and four white ones.

4 Use your pencil and ruler to draw a line .5 cm (¼ in.) in from each side on the wrong side of one of the fabric squares. These will be your sewing lines. Repeat this step for each square.

5 On a table, line up a blue square, a white square and another blue square. This will be your first row.

6 For the second row, line up a white square, a blue square and another white square.

7 Your third row will be the same as the first row. Your squares should be alternating blue and white. (See the illustration on the facing page.)

8 With the right sides together, pin the first blue square to the white square beside it.

9 With the needle and thread, use a running stitch (as shown on the facing page) to stitch the squares together along the sewing lines. Remove the pins as you sew.

10 Now sew the other blue square to the centre white square.

11 Use this same method to stitch together the squares in the other two rows.

12 Ask an adult to help you press the seams toward the blue fabric in each row.

blue	white	blue
white	blue	white
blue	white	blue

Nine Patch Block: The diagonal position of the blue blocks is the start of the Irish Chain quilt.

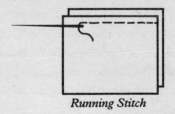

Running Stitch

13 With the right sides together, sew the top row to the middle row, and the bottom row to the other two rows. Press the seams smooth.

14 You now have a nine-patch block. See the author's Web site **http://www.barbarahaworthattard.com** for how to make your block part of an Irish chain quilt, or you can make a pillow out of your block.

To make a pillow

Place your block face down on the right side of another piece of cotton. Trace the block and cut out the large fabric square. (Or you can make a second block to use for the back of the pillow.) With the right sides together, pin and stitch the front and back together on three sides. Remove the pins as you sew. Turn the pillow right side out and stuff it with a pillow form. Tuck in the raw edges and stitch the pillow closed.